BEHIND HIS EYES

CONSEQUENCES

A CONSEQUENCES SERIES READING COMPANION
Book #1.5 of the bestselling Consequences Series

Aleatha Romig

New York Times and USA Today
bestselling author

Behind His Eyes—Consequences
Published by Aleatha Romig
2014 Edition

Copyright ©2013 Aleatha Romig

ISBN 13: 978-0988489196
ISBN 10: 0988489198

Editing: Lisa Aurello
Formatting: Angela McLaurin – Fictional Formats

Acknowledgements

Thank you to everyone who has made my story real! Thank you for your support and devotion. I'm constantly awed by your dedication to Tony and Claire. If it weren't for your questions and messages, I would never have continued with these reading companions.

Thank you for encouraging me to experience the other side of the Consequences!

Disclaimer

---◆---

The CONSEQUENCES series contains dark adult content. Although there is not excessive use of description and detail, the content contains innuendos of kidnapping, rape, and abuse—both physical and mental. If you're unable to read this material, please do not purchase. If you are ready, welcome aboard and enjoy the ride!

~Aleatha Romig

Note From Aleatha

Dear Readers,

Before purchasing, please understand that this is *not* a standalone book. It was not meant to be read independently of THE CONSEQUENCES SERIES. It was meant as a *companion,* to be read following the experience of the ENTIRE CONSEQUENCES SERIES.

This was not designed as a *retell* of the entire novel CONSEQUENCES from Anthony Rawlings' perspective and as such, will not make sense on its own. It was meant to share significant scenes and behind-the-scenes information.

Therefore, *after* you have completed CONSEQUENCES, TRUTH, CONVICTED, REVEALED, and BEYOND THE CONSEQUENCES please join me for a dark journey into the mind of a man who believes that he controls everything and controls nothing.

Join me for an insight into the man who...

Once upon a time, signed a napkin that he knew was a contract. As an esteemed businessman, he forgot one very important rule—he forgot to read the fine print. It wasn't an acquisition to own another person as he'd previously assumed. It was an agreement to acquire a soul.
—Aleatha Romig, CONVICTED

This companion centers on CONSEQUENCES and includes chapter references to that novel. The end of this companion also contains a glossary of characters and a timeline of significant events in CONSEQUENCES. BEHIND HIS EYES—TRUTH is also available. The glossary and timeline will grow with each companion.

Thank you again for your support!

~Aleatha

BEHIND HIS EYES

CONSEQUENCES

A CONSEQUENCES SERIES READING COMPANION
Book #1.5 of the bestselling Consequences Series

*The tragic or the humorous is a
matter of perspective.
—Arnold Beisser*

Aleatha Romig

Prologue

Before the beginning—fall 2004

---

*Men may know many things by seeing; but no prophet can
see before the event, nor what end waits for him.*
—Sophocles

ANTHONY RAWLINGS' PRIVATE jet soared east toward Indiana. Looking
around the cabin, he took in the empty seats. It wasn't often that he
flew alone. Most of his travels were business-related, and he had
assistants, negotiators, and legal counsel who usually accompanied
him. This trip was different—sudden, unexpected, and confidential.
The only person who knew of this trip was his pilot and trusted
employee, Eric. He wouldn't discuss the business of this trip with
anyone; of that, Anthony was confident. There were other aspects of
the journey that didn't leave him as secure.

Throughout the years, Anthony had become a public figure and
had a reputation that needed to be upheld. To that end, he surrounded
himself with the best—the best people, business decisions, and
belongings. Rarely did Anthony Rawlings act impulsively. Every move
was considered, debated, and evaluated—yet this trip could qualify as
impetuous. He never considered flying to Indiana until he received the

phone call informing him of the automobile accident claiming the lives of Jordon and Shirley Nichols. Truthfully, even now, the trip wasn't necessary. He'd told the private investigator who'd called to attend the funeral and take pictures; nonetheless, as he hung up the telephone, Anthony knew that wouldn't be enough.

He'd been observing Claire Nichols from afar for over a year. Enjoying the freedom that comes with seclusion, Anthony leafed through the most recent report from the PI for the umpteenth time. It contained pictures of Claire—lots of pictures. He couldn't pinpoint his curiosity regarding this girl; after all, she was just a child—merely a sophomore in college! Catherine called it an obsession, and more than once, she claimed that it was unhealthy. She reminded him that the names on their list needed to remain just that—names, not people. That sounded good in principle, and for most on their list, it was possible. Claire Nichols was different. He found himself drawn to her, wanting to know more; however, Anthony wouldn't classify his interest as an *obsession*—it was more of a *diversion*.

In real life, he had a lot on his plate. Rawlings Industries was doing well, very well. He had more than enough to keep him busy. Claire Nichols was something of a fantasy, his *distraction,* like an exhibit at the zoo. Perhaps that was a bad analogy. Animals at the zoo can only be watched. At first, that was what he did with the Nichols girls: he watched. Then, with time, he experimented. *What good is having money if you can't use it to your enjoyment?* He wanted to know if he could influence the lives on their list. Emily Nichols didn't hold the draw that, somehow, her younger sister possessed; therefore, he made a few calls and learned some information. With his connections, it wasn't difficult to take that information and change the course of history. A call here, another there, and suddenly, Claire's suitor had an amazing intern opportunity across the country. It was exhilarating and proved that Anthony could manipulate Claire's world.

She was young, vivacious, and attractive; he doubted that his impact thus far would prove significant, but it proved that without a doubt, he could influence the course of her life. That knowledge was intoxicating and addicting. He continually wondered how far he could go.

As the saying went, knowledge was power, and Anthony Rawlings thrived on power. In everyday life, he had the power to change lives— those of employees and the futures of companies. Claire Nichols was unlike those decisions made from behind the desk as a CEO. Altering her life was done covertly, without Claire's knowledge. The risk of discovery added to his elation.

Placing the most recent photos of Claire into a file folder and securing them in his briefcase, Anthony closed his eyes. The ever-present voice that worked day and night pushing his inner drive for success began to fill his thoughts. There were times that Anthony yearned for the real live, breathing mentor who'd influenced his life in such a dramatic way, but that wasn't possible. His grandfather, Nathaniel Rawls, had been taken from him and from the rest of his family by the workings of seemingly inconsequential people—people who had changed the Rawls family forever. Not only did they change it—they eliminated it. The name Rawls ceased to exist.

It was a favor Anthony Rawlings intended to return.

Nathaniel's voice echoed in his thoughts... words that Anthony would never forget, words that were aimed toward both Sherman Nichols and Jonathon Burke. *Not just them—hell, no. They took away my world. They took my family. Their damn kids, their kids, and their kids' kids... they'll all face the consequences of their actions!*

That promise was spoken by the once powerful entrepreneurial giant who'd been reduced to nothing more than a common prisoner. Nathaniel's threat repeated as a constant cadence in Anthony's life, often accompanied by the shame now associated with his birth name. Public shame—failure for the world to see, all of it brought on by those individuals. Anthony had been born a Rawls—Anton Rawls. He longed for his current success to honor the name his grandfather wore proudly as a soldier and a businessman; however, that homage would never be. Each time he penned the name *Anthony Rawlings* on a contract, a completed business deal, or a monumental acquisition, he'd recall his grandfather's words, and the roots of Nathaniel's final desire would plunge deeper into his being. Those roots were now so ingrained and intertwined that they completed one another. He didn't know when it had become so consuming, yet it filled so much of him—had pushed away other desires and feelings—until Anthony couldn't imagine his life without the vendetta. It wasn't debatable; Nathaniel's wish would be fulfilled. Without fulfilling Nathaniel's wish, Anthony Rawlings would be incomplete.

Anthony didn't ask for the rewind reel of Nathaniel's voice, which continually ran through his subconscious, and he didn't need it. No, he had an everyday living, breathing reminder of his obligation—his grandfather's second wife. Perhaps, without Anthony realizing, she was wise with her words. She never told Anthony that he *failed* his grandfather; instead, she'd subtly remind him that he had *yet* to succeed. Although her impatience grated on him, she was one of the few people Anthony allowed to fully voice her thoughts—especially when it involved his decisions. He overlooked her redundancy, because she too had lost everything. Anthony knew that if it weren't for him, she'd have lost more, but the truth stared at him with steel-gray eyes almost every day. It was his failure in controlling his father's vengeance that cost Nathaniel's wife dearly.

Overlooking her reminders was Anthony's penitence. He'd promised Nathaniel that he would look after Marie. If he'd succeeded in stopping his father's retaliation, things could have been different. When Marie lost her last name, Anthony failed Nathaniel. He also failed his parents the night they died. He wouldn't fail Nathaniel again.

The way Anthony reasoned, his planning, or procrastination as Marie called it, regarding the vendetta had paid off. Although he allowed her prompts for retaliation, he also reminded her that Anthony Rawlings worked on his own schedule and towards his own goals. Their list of *children* had grown shorter by the day through natural attrition. Jonathon Burke and his wife, Sherman Nichols and his wife, and now Jordon Nichols and his wife were gone. The original two and their wives passed away of natural causes. He had provided the funds to watch their health fail from afar, but his true interest lay in observing their children and their children. The PI explained that wet leaves were believed to be involved in Jordon and Shirley Nichols' automobile crash. Anthony didn't care about the cause, as long as he could cross them off their list. Now, his concern centered on the next generation.

As the plane touched down, his anticipation built... instead of pictures and reports, he would, for the first time, see Emily and Claire Nichols in person.

In an effort to minimize his visibility, Anthony dressed down and walked to the back of the church's sanctuary. It didn't take long for him to realize he could easily be lost in the crowd. The Nichols had been well-respected members of their community, and the church was overflowing with mourners. He'd never been to a funeral with so many people willing to speak. Apparently, Jordon had been a first-rate policeman; the church was wall-to-wall with uniformed officers. Shirley had also been a well-loved teacher. As the afternoon wore on, Anthony couldn't help but watch Claire. She was seated next to her sister, and often, the two held onto one another's hands. That wasn't what captivated him. What caught his attention was how Emily had the man to her left. Anthony knew he was John Vandersol, Emily's longtime boyfriend. Occasionally, Emily would break down and John would console her. Claire, on the other hand, remained steadfast. The pain was visible in her expression, yet only occasionally did she bow her head or wipe her eyes. Her stoic veneer fascinated him. *Was she truly that strong? What were her limits? Could she be broken?*

Anthony assumed that if he hadn't lured Simon Johnson away to California, the young man would be present to offer Claire his shoulder. That had been Anthony's first attempt to manipulate her life, and it had been too easy. He would continue to look for more opportunities.

The preacher spoke, countless people gave their condolences, but Anthony's mind was on Claire's future. As he watched her, he thought about all he knew. He didn't know how long her future would last; however, he did know that it was now at his discretion, and in some way, he would be a part of it.

The first step would be the scholarship at Valparaiso; it would be necessary for her to complete her degree. He'd already started the groundwork. After all, he'd originally assumed that he'd be at the Nichols' funeral due to more manipulation. The fact that the vengeance gods looked down and blessed his plans reinforced his determination.

After the service concluded, the caskets were wheeled down the center aisle followed by the family. The church was a murmur of whispers as organ music played from somewhere above. Anthony couldn't suppress his curiosity as Emily, John, and Claire headed his direction. Soon, they would pass mere feet away. If he reached past the older gentleman on his left, he could seize Claire's hand; however, he knew that couldn't happen, even though, as she moved toward him, she had already paused a few times to hold a mourner's hand and accept his or her condolences. It wouldn't look right; Anthony didn't look sad. He wasn't heartbroken over the loss—no, he was intrigued.

Then, just as the family neared, the man on Anthony's left reached forward and spoke. "Emily and Claire, please know how sorry I am for your loss."

They stopped and each young lady reached out and hugged the older gentleman. It was Claire who responded, "Thank you for coming. I know Dad and Mom would have loved to have seen you." Her voice was strong despite the burden of her loss.

"You know that I wouldn't have missed…"

Anthony didn't listen to the man's words. He was mesmerized by the green eyes he saw before him. He'd seen them in photographs—he had a whole file. They were different in person, more vivid, alive, and so full of emotion. Sadness prevailed, yet there was something else, Drive? Ambition? Determination? He wanted to gaze longer into their depths, but before he could speak and offer his condolences, Emily smiled sadly at the gentleman and the three were gone.

It was there, in that church, in Indianapolis, Indiana, that Anthony resolved that his and Claire's paths would cross again. Someday he'd learn just how strong she could be in the face of greater adversity.

Chapter 1

Tardiness has Consequences—April 2010

(Consequences—Chapter 5)

———◆———

To know the rules of the game, you have to be educated.
—L.L. Cool J.

MINDLESSLY, THE PAD of Anthony's thumb ran laps around the smooth rim of the crystal tumbler. He wasn't thinking about the glass in his hand or even the Evan Williams bourbon swirling near the bottom. No, Anthony's thoughts were centered on the monitors above his grand desk. From multiple, well-placed cameras, he could watch Claire move about the S.E suite.

During his time in Europe, the appeal of the woman held captive in his home had begun to fade. In all honesty, having acquired his goal, his return home seemed somewhat anticlimactic. After all, the hunt had taken years, and with each bit of new information, and each time he manipulated fate, Anthony felt invigorated. For a long time, Anthony had known that one day his target would be his.

The capture was all that he'd imagined and more—the true climax! From the moment he stepped into the Red Wing, Anthony knew he'd succeed. He was, first and foremost, a businessman with an impeccable record of success, especially when an endeavor had his full commitment. Whether in business or in pleasure, Anthony understood that planning and patience were essential elements for success. Before embarking on any deal, Anthony Rawlings thoroughly assessed the situation, eliminated the risks, and accentuated the assets.

This acquisition was different. Unlike the average acquisition, such as one of a company, *this* acquisition had risks that he couldn't avoid. Sometimes that happened in the game of chance. The first risk was his public interaction with Claire; sitting with her in the Red Wing and taking her out to dinner were undoubtedly perilous. After all, he's well-known, and the possibility of being associated, even coincidentally, with a missing person wouldn't fit his perfect persona.

In all reality, he could have paid for Claire Nichols' disappearance—only to have her reappear in his home—but that would've increased the number of people privy to his plan. With her ultimate future unsure, Anthony felt the fewer number of people on that list, the better. Most importantly, if he'd paid someone to bring her to Iowa, he would've missed out on the euphoria that came with finalizing the *big deal*. Anthony had experienced that feeling over and over in business, but that was nothing like the sensation of slipping the GHB into Claire's wine glass. At that moment, he knew that there was no turning back—he didn't want to.

Being a professional businessman with an image to maintain, Anthony worked out every possible scenario and created believable contingency plans. The time and energy he'd put into Claire Nichols' acquisition could have been billed in millions—literally. Anthony Rawlings' time was incredibly valuable. Suddenly, his lips twitched upward. *Perhaps he should add his billable hours in planning and executing Claire's acquisition to Claire's bill? But, wouldn't that be like a jail sentence of 'life' plus 1000 years? Her first debt was practically insurmountable; adding more to it was truly adding insult to injury.*

Movement on the screen caused him to refocus. He watched as Claire unsuccessfully tried to open a bottle of water. After a few attempts she wiped her hands on the arms of the chair and finally removed the cap. If he'd have zoomed closer, he would've seen her complexion pale as she forced herself to swallow the refreshing liquid. Satisfaction filled his chest; his delay was working—Claire knew he was coming to her, and her anxiety was obviously growing with each passing minute.

Maybe—just maybe—he'd been wrong to think the fun was over. Perhaps there'd be more opportunities to enjoy the woman in the black dress and heels he was watching. He reminded himself, it wasn't all about enjoyment, well at least not hers. No, Claire Nichols had a bill to pay and lessons to learn.

Anthony was in a place he'd never been. Metaphorically, he was entering virgin territory. After all, he'd never before held a woman captive. There'd never been a need—or a desire. Women were a nice accessory and a necessary complement for many occasions, and through the years, more women than he could remember were willing to fulfill that role, as well as be attentive to his physical needs. Of course, he treated each one with respect. Anthony Rawlings couldn't have disgruntled women running around talking about him in a negative way. Each separation was his fault—*his* plate was too full, *he* had too many responsibilities. The fact that he usually dated high-profile women helped. They, too, had lives, responsibilities, and reputations that required discretion. If he tried to remember half of the gorgeous women he'd dated, Anthony believed that all of his separations had ended amicably.

Thankfully, he had people like Shelly, his publicist, and Patricia, his private assistant, to remind him when he'd be encountering an old flame. It even seemed that at times, Patricia found his lack of sincerity regarding these women amusing. After all, many of them, at one time or another, considered him a boyfriend. The reality couldn't be farther from the truth. Never in forty-five years had Anthony Rawlings considered himself someone's *boyfriend*. The concept was laughable.

It wasn't that he didn't enjoy the company of women; it was that, in the game of life, women were a liability, a risk that he wasn't willing to take. He was a master at appearances. Accepting a woman as anything more than an accessory for an evening or as an outlet for physical needs would be to allow that woman to be part of his persona—part of his life. That had never happened, nor did Anthony Rawlings foresee it happening in the future. He had too much at stake.

Bringing his thoughts back to Claire, he felt a renewed sense of anticipation. New experiences were rare for him. Viewing the monitors as Claire pretended to read—since she hadn't turned the page in over ten minutes, he knew she wasn't concentrating—he conceded that undoubtedly this would be a brand-new experience. He just had to figure out exactly what he would do with it—and with her. His grin reemerged.

Oh, he knew what he would do with her—whatever he wanted. The question that loomed in his mind was how she would respond. Although she'd willingly engaged in vanilla sex in Atlanta, since coming to Iowa, she'd been considerably less compliant; however, Anthony reminded himself, that was before—before her nearly two week *time-out*. After watching the short interaction between Catherine and Claire on the video recording, when Catherine informed her of his impending arrival, Anthony believed Claire had experienced an attitude adjustment.

Truly, he didn't know how he wanted her to react when he entered the suite. The fact she was dressed appropriately held potential. Perhaps she could be trained to work off not only her bill, but the un-payable invoice that included the life of his grandfather—*and* perhaps some of his own billable time.

Briefly, Anthony changed a section of the screen to the Atlanta news. He'd been watching and scanning it daily during his travels in Europe. After over two weeks in his possession, he was happy to see that there hadn't been any news reports or voiced concerns about the disappearance of Claire Nichols. It appeared as though Anthony's efforts had paid off—emails, text messages, and Facebook messages all accomplished their goal. Claire's friends and family believed she'd left town to pursue a new job opportunity—Anthony grinned as he switched the screen back to the S.E. suite—and their beliefs were in essence true. *This* was and would be her new job. Momentarily, he closed his eyes, as mental images of Claire's growing list of *job* responsibilities filled his thoughts. *Perhaps he should compile a written list?*

A knock at his office door pulled Anthony from his sinister thoughts.

With a click of his mouse, the screens turned from the monitors in the S.E. suite to the closing stock market results for Rawlings Industries and its plethora of subsidiaries. Without inquiring, Anthony hit the button to allow access to his domain. It was after 9:00 PM and this was *his* home. He didn't need to inquire as to who was about to enter his inner sanctuary; there were few possibilities.

"Mr. Rawlings, did you want to see me?" Catherine's voice echoed as she stepped into Anthony's office. Once the door was shut, she lifted a brow. "I would've thought you'd have investigated yourself, Anton."

"I plan to. First, I want to know a few things."

Catherine perched herself on the edge of a chair near his desk. "You weren't watching from your trip?"

"I was, but there are some things you can't decipher from a video feed—such as attitude. Tell me about the last two weeks; how have they been?"

Catherine smiled. "Educational. I happened to look inside the suite a few minutes ago. Did you see what she's wearing?"

"I did. Did you tell her what to wear?"

"No, I told her that it was up to her."

Anthony nodded as he sat back against his leather chair. "So, she seems to understand the importance of appearance—that's good. What about interaction?"

"Until today, since you left, she's only had access to Carlos. He delivered all her meals and returned for the dishes. The rest of the staff entered only when she was occupied with her showers."

Anthony grinned. "Carlos—Carlos doesn't speak English, at least not well."

"I know."

"Very good, Catherine, I applaud your resourcefulness."

"Thank you, Anton. I may not agree with your plan; however, I told you I'd do my part. Now, what do you expect when you enter the suite?"

"What do I expect? I expect respect for the authority I obviously hold over every aspect of her life. At this moment, I expect her to have the good sense to recognize the magnitude of her current situation."

Catherine leaned forward, her voice held the tone of a warning. "Caged animals fight. I saw the scratches on your arms when she first arrived."

"That won't happen again."

"And you're sure of this?"

Anthony nodded confidently. "I am." He wondered if Catherine would ask for more clarification. If she had, he wasn't sure he'd share his plans. After all, those plans were why his excitement at their reunion was once again growing. Anthony glanced at his watch. "Did you tell her I'd be there at 10:00 PM?"

"I told her between 9:00 PM and 10:00 PM. She seemed desperate for me to stay and talk. I believe she's lonely."

"I saw that on the video." The woman he'd observed in Atlanta was both social in her work and her private life. Perhaps this time away from others *was* beneficial. He planned to emphasize how he controlled her interactions. His grin broke through his facade with the realization—*there wouldn't be anything he didn't control.*

"Thank you, Catherine. I think I can handle this from here."

She stood. "This was very risky for a man of your—"

"Thank you, Catherine," he interrupted. "It's a roll of the dice. High risks yield the best results. It's about time I learn if your manipulation has added to my yields."

Before stepping from the room, Catherine smiled. "I'm sure you'll capitalize on your investment... Mr. Rawlings."

Anthony looked at his watch again, 9:51 PM. One last click of his mouse and he saw Claire, up on the screen, pacing near the fireplace in her suite. There wasn't anything he didn't know about her, from her family to her medical history. He knew that she and her sister were all that remained of the Sherman Nichols line. He also knew that she liked her coffee with cream, and that about six months ago, Claire had had the birth control device inserted. During his observations, he didn't find her to be promiscuous; the doctor's notations stated something about *convenience*. Grinning toward the screen, Anthony agreed: the insert was convenient.

Standing, Anthony put on and buttoned his double-breasted suit jacket. *No, he'd been wrong when he thought the actual acquisition had been the climax—there would definitely be many more to come!*

Anthony depressed the button on the side of the doorframe while simultaneously hearing the *beep* and opening the door. Claire's eyes opened wide while she remained seated in the chair near the fireplace. The last time he'd seen her—in person—she'd looked like hell, wearing a robe, her hair a mess, and her face discolored. Tonight was definitely an improvement. It wasn't just her appearance, although Anthony approved; it was her demeanor. That morning, nearly two weeks ago, Claire had been out of control—demanding, yelling, and crying. It wasn't that she was in control now; Anthony saw the fear in her eyes. It was that she was... composed.

"Good evening, Claire."

She stood and replied, "Good evening, Anthony. Shall we sit?"

When he stepped toward her, he noticed her quick intake of air. Confidently, he sat on the sofa, leaned back, and unbuttoned his jacket. He watched intently as she sat on the edge of the chair with her back straight. The *hum* of the fireplace fan filled the room as he considered the woman before him. Without a doubt, she was an improvement over the one he'd left on the floor of the same suite.

He waited to see if she would ramble. When only the fireplace blower prevailed, Anthony spoke, "Do you think you're ready to continue with our agreement? Or do you need some more time alone to consider the situation?"

"After consulting my attorney, I feel I have no choice but to continue with our agreement."

Anthony felt the hairs on the back of his neck stand to attention. *What the hell?* He glared toward the woman who had the audacity to sound trite. "Claire, I know you're joking, but do you really think it's a good idea? Considering your circumstances?"

"I've had a lot of time to think; joviality has sustained me."

He tilted his head. *The woman had nerve—he'd give her that.* "I must say your demeanor impresses me. I'll need to deliberate on this new personality."

He sat silently and contemplated this petite woman who had the fortitude to maintain eye contact, and answer his questions with a hint of bravado, all while knowing she was at his mercy. *Or did she know? Did she think this was some kind of sick reality TV show and any minute it would be over?* He stared. "Tell me what you've learned during your reflection time."

She rambled about clothes and food, truly inconsequential things. Anthony interrupted, "That's all very nice, but what have you discovered about your situation?" He couldn't contain his condescending tone, perhaps he didn't want to. After all, she needed to know who held the answers. "Do you even know where you are?"

After only a moment's hesitation, she said, "I'm in Iowa, or at least somewhere near Iowa City."

How the hell? He'd scanned hours of video—did someone pass her a note of some kind? Anthony couldn't imagine that they'd disrespect him like that. "And... you learned this... from whom?"

"I learned it from the *Weather Channel—Local on the Eights.* The local weather for this area comes from Iowa City, Iowa."

Anthony exhaled. *Damn, he was on edge. Her flippant attitude needed readjustment.* "Very well, that will spare me telling you. For the sake of clarity, since that seemed to be a problem in the past, you're aware that your indebtedness *to me* can only be determined paid *by me*?"

Her smile appeared pained, yet she managed to keep it in place as she nodded. Anthony waited for an answer. When she didn't speak, he proclaimed, "I prefer verbal confirmation."

"I am aware that you are the only one who can decide when my debt is paid in full." Though her words sounded too calm, her hands remained clenched. She'd never know how that unconscious act helped to calm her captor. He wanted—no needed—to know that she understood his authority.

He continued, "You are also aware that your duties require you to be available to me whenever, wherever, and however I demand?" His eyes never left hers.

"I am aware."

He reiterated for clarification. "You're aware that you must at all times obey my rules?"

"I'm aware that I must do as I'm told."

She was good. He didn't believe a damn word she said, but he had to admit, she was good. Oh, he considered demonstrating more of his authority, but perhaps Catherine had been right. Claire Nichols was lonely, and she was grasping at the straws of *any* interaction. Perhaps no interaction would prove to be the most educational tool. Besides, he had plenty of time—as much as he wanted—for interaction. Finally, he spoke, "Very well." He stood and walked toward the door.

Before he reached his destination, Claire's determined tone rang throughout the suite. "Wait."

Anthony turned, unable to hide the shock at her demand, his eyes locked onto hers.

Apparently, she had the good sense to realize her breach of station. Immediately, her tone softened, "I'm sorry... but may I leave this suite?"

Apologetic and requesting permission—yes, Anthony could deal with that. "As long as we are certain on the terms of our agreement, and you follow the rules and orders given, I see no problem with your roaming the house." He reached for the door handle. "It's rather large. I'll be working from home tomorrow. Your services will be utilized then, so be prepared for my call. When I have a chance, I'll give you a tour of the house and define your limitations. I think it's best that you don't roam tonight. I don't want you getting lost." Within his pocket, he depressed the sensor, causing the *beep* to sound once again. Anthony reached for the handle.

"Anthony?" The earlier strength he'd heard in her tone was gone. "I don't have any... *duties* tonight?"

"I've recently arrived from a series of meetings in Europe and am quite tired. I'm glad to know we have a mutual understanding. Goodnight, Claire."

As he shut her door, he heard her say goodnight.

Walking toward his office, he thought about the bourbon he'd left sitting on his desk—there were about fifty emails that needed reading and probably responses to be written—and he had at least two web conferences tomorrow. He'd need to check to see if Patricia had sent him his schedule.

Oh, yes, and apparently his *acquisition* was adapting to her new reality—that was good. Anthony Rawlings had too many things to think about other than to be concerned with the woman upstairs. Hell, Catherine had been spot-on with the isolation. Perhaps he should allow her to deal with the day-to-day maintenance; he'd utilize Claire when it fit his schedule. Besides, a little alone time seemed to be just what the doctor ordered.

Damn, in a week and a half the proposal from Arkansas was coming in. Did he have that preliminary report? There were too many other things to think about besides Claire Nichols; however, it was comforting to know she'd adapted. Tomorrow, Anthony decided he'd take that theory to the next level. *Would her actions be as accommodating as her words?*

———————⸺◆⸺———————

THE MORNING LIGHT had yet to penetrate the heavy drapes of his suite when Anthony turned toward the red numbers. It was only 4:42 AM, yet he was wide awake. The woman—about whom, he reminded himself, he didn't give a damn—was inside his house. She was undoubtedly sleeping soundly under *his* roof. *How many nights had he imagined what it would be like to have her where he could watch her, train her, and control her?* Now she was here and he was a floor away. If he went upstairs and took what his body obviously wanted, what difference would it make? This wasn't a normal dating scenario.

Claire wasn't going to go to the press and proclaim his actions. She wasn't going anywhere. Besides, this wasn't about sex, although he was painfully erect. It was about power. Everything about her existence was his to determine. If he wanted her to sleep, she would sleep. If he wanted to use her, he would use her.

Though the thought of entering her suite—no, not *her* suite, the *S.E.* suite—and asserting his dominance while assessing her reaction appealed to him, Anthony reconsidered: the more accommodating he made her, the better. He didn't relish the idea of continued daily battles. Yes, he liked things his way; however, his energies could be better utilized if she were more compliant.

Catherine was right. Showing up to the office with scratches on his face or arms would instigate questions. Making his way out of bed, Anthony walked to his bureau, opened the top drawer, and found what he'd purchased in Europe. Running the long lengths of black satin across his palm, his mind considered the possibilities of their use. It wasn't that he was into the kinky shit; this was more about self-preservation. He could even consider it a favor. Claire's fighting hadn't worked well for her in the past, and he wouldn't allow it in the future. With the use of satin restraints, he would assure that when he exited the S.E. suite, he'd be scathe-free, and with her cooperation, albeit forced, Claire would be able to boast the same.

In his mind, he was giving her a choice. She would accommodate him; how much independence she had while doing that would be up to her.

A little after 7:00 AM, Anthony scaled the grand staircase. He hadn't acted upon his earlier thoughts of Claire; instead, he'd gone to the pool, swam laps, and lifted weights for an hour. After a shower and breakfast, he decided to spend some time preparing for his web conferences. As he read, each sentence disappeared into the memories of the innocent emerald-green gaze from last night, the one that asked,

I'm sorry... but may I leave this suite?

He wasn't concerned about fulfilling her desires. It was basic psychology: operant conditioning—positive consequences for positive behavior, negative consequences for negative behavior. Her respectful tone, her demeanor, and her appearance—they all deserved a positive consequence. *After all, wasn't that what he wanted to do—to promote the positive and rebuke the negative?*

He also remembered telling her to be ready in the morning. *Would she be? Did she truly deserve a positive consequence?*

The *beep* sounded as he moved silently into the S.E suite. Scanning the room, Claire was nowhere to be found. His first thought was the bathroom, but the door was ajar and no one was there. Before he could look further, he heard movement from the closet/dressing room. Staring in that direction, he waited for her to emerge. When she did, the startled *yelp*, accompanied by the dropping of her shoes, made his cheeks rise. "Good morning, Claire." She was ready—*another reason for a positive consequence.*

"Good morning, Anthony; I didn't hear you come in."

Amused, he watched as she picked up her shoes and feigned calmness. It was then he noticed her uneaten breakfast on the table. "Are you ready for your tour? Did you plan to eat first? I have a web conference in forty-five minutes."

She asked him about a web conference. As he answered, he had difficulty suppressing his amusement at her behavior. It was as if carrying on a mundane conversation with the man who held her future in his hands was an everyday occurrence. Snickering to himself, he reasoned, *it will be from now on.* Maybe she was working from her years as a bartender. Whatever the cause, her ability to converse effortlessly was a welcome surprise. Before long, Anthony found himself leading her down corridors and describing the estate. As he discussed pieces of furniture and fine works of art, he knew that there was no way Claire could know the items he pointed out were originally owned by his grandfather. She didn't know that it had taken Anthony years to track down significant pieces of his history, after they'd been auctioned off to undeserving bidders. She also couldn't know how the mention of each item fortified his resolve for restitution; instead, Claire walked beside him, blissfully unaware. A saying about a spider and a fly came to mind.

They were in the library when she asked something about computers. He didn't know if she were joking about the size of the library and the magnitude of books, yet her comment hit him wrong. Suddenly, Anthony felt the need to remind her of her status. She may be receiving a tour that few others had experienced, but she wasn't a guest, and he wanted to make that clear. "I think it would be best for you to not have access to computers, the Internet, or telephones." Oh, he wanted a verbal response; however, the unspoken acknowledgement of his authority that flooded her eyes momentarily satisfied that need. He silently vowed that they would discuss the need for verbal responses in the future.

She didn't speak again until they entered the indoor pool. Anthony never gave the room much thought—it was a pool. There were windows, tile, and water. Yet as they entered, Claire gasped. He responded before he had a chance to think. "Do you like to swim?"

"Oh, yes. This is amazing."

"You shall have bathing suits tomorrow." As soon as the words left his lips, Anthony wondered why he'd been so forthcoming. She hadn't asked and that was his rule—requests must be made before they can be granted; nevertheless, he'd approved an unspoken request. He would follow through, because he was a man of his word, but he didn't intend to offer more. The tour *and* bathing suits—her positive rewards were outnumbering her behaviors.

At the entrance to his office, Anthony realized the time and proclaimed, "I have business I must do. It's 7:25 AM. I want you back at my office at 10:30 AM. You have some debt to pay." He watched for her reaction. It wasn't overt, but her eyes momentarily drifted toward the wall. To her credit she recovered quickly. He asked, "Do you think you can find your way back to your suite?"

It was then that she did it again. Her voice softened as she asked permission to go to the library. *As long as she stayed in the library and returned to his office at 10:30 AM, what harm was there in allowing her request?* Besides, it was a *request*—well worded. While reiterating the importance of her returning at the appropriate time, he apprehensively acquiesced; however, before he dismissed her, he reminded her of his control. "We have not discussed all of the rules pertaining to the house. At this point, do not go outside. Permission for going out on the grounds will be contingent upon your ability to follow rules within the house."

Anthony liked how she bristled at the mention of her restrictions. Yes, he had thousands of jobs and people's livelihoods in his hands, but never had he had one person's life completely in his grasp. He had to admit, the power was intense and even erotic.

Anthony watched the clock as the web conference dragged on. When he finally disconnected, he looked at the time. Claire was due in his office in six minutes. Anthony clicked a few times with his mouse and entered a code. His screen filled with a view of the library. It didn't take long to find Claire wandering about, pulling out books, and reading the backs. He waited and watched as she opened a book and leaned against a bookcase. The numbers on the clock changed. *Didn't she realize the size of his house?* There was no possible way, unless she ran, that she would make it to his office in time. *Did she think he was joking about returning on time?* She didn't even have the good sense to turn toward the library clock.

At 10:37 AM he entered the library. This time, Anthony found no humor in the fact he'd again startled her. She was stupid to even think that she could blatantly disobey him. He'd provided positive consequences—obviously it wasn't enough to mold the appropriate behavior. When her eyes met his, he saw the remorse.

"Oh, Anthony, I'm so sorry. I was just engrossed in all you have—"

Excuses! He didn't make them and he didn't listen to them. His hand struck her cheek. Before she could look away, Anthony seized the back of her neck and pulled her eyes toward his. "Simple instructions, which are what I gave you—perhaps you're not ready to leave your suite quite yet."

He heard her plea—telling him that she *could* follow instructions. Her words didn't match her actions, and he didn't have the time or the patience for coddling.

"Follow me to my office—now." Not waiting for her to respond, he took off through the library and down the corridor. With each step he contemplated his next move, reminding himself that this was a critical time in Claire's training. *If he didn't demonstrate his dominance now, he couldn't guarantee her compliance later. Didn't she understand that this was for her own good? This arrangement would never last if she didn't cooperate, and then what would his options be? She needed to recognize his authority!*

By the time they reached the grand doors to his office, red infiltrated his vision. It wasn't intense, but the world had a crimson hue. Catherine had told him that he was wrong to take Claire. Nathaniel's plan had been clear, yet there was something about Claire that fascinated him. He wouldn't fail and prove Catherine right. He *would* make Claire behave appropriately—this *would* work.

Shoving her inside his office, Anthony reeled in the red and spoke in his most even tone. "So, you say you *can* follow instructions. We'll see." He watched as she stood before him trembling. He wondered how she could be trembling—his anger warmed him to an uncomfortable heat. Then he realized, it wasn't cold: it was fear. That was good. Fear was an excellent motivator. He continued, "Let's start with you taking off your clothes."

Though her hands shook as she unfastened the clasps, she didn't argue. Whenever she looked away, he reached for her chin and redirected her eyes. There was so much he could see in her eyes; he refused to allow her to hide that emotion. After he redirected her the second time, she maintained eye contact. Once she was nude, he assessed. There was nothing wrong with her body. She'd even seemed to have lost some weight since she first arrived. Her earlier markings were gone, and her skin tone was lighter—probably due to staying inside. After all, she wasn't in the warm Georgia sun any longer.

"Lie down on the floor," he directed.

She didn't speak, yet he saw her indecision. Anthony Rawlings wouldn't make the same request twice. Just as he was about to assist, Claire knelt on the carpet.

"Lie on your stomach and keep your face and eyes down."

He didn't know if it was his imagination or if time was indeed moving slowly; nevertheless, each of her movements seemed to occur painfully slow. *At least they were occurring.* Despite the fact that she was still trembling, she eventually lay down, totally nude, and prone on the carpet.

Anthony had had his fair share of experiences in life; however, this was once again entering the world of new and untested territory. He'd accepted the responsibility to train this woman, to make her into a compliant soul. Catherine said it couldn't be done. She said that women today were too independent. Watching Claire lie as still as possible, Anthony almost laughed—*independent indeed.* Claire Nichols would learn to behave.

Perhaps it was a childhood memory, or maybe something he'd read; regardless of the source, physical negative reinforcement was often very effective in molding behavior. Even Pavlov's dog learned to *stop* responding to the bell once the reinforcement turned from food to an electrical shock. Claire Nichols would learn to listen to Anthony. When she replied appropriately, she earned house tours and time in the library. When she disappointed him, she earned negative reinforcement.

Slowly, Anthony unbuckled his belt. It wasn't the fulfillment of the punishment he sought. No, it was Claire's reaction. He needed to hear her response. When his belt contacted her back for the first blow, she let out a satisfying scream. It was his reinforcement, confirming her understanding of his control. That scream told Anthony that she understood her behavior was unacceptable. He wanted more.

He listened as the belt contacted her skin—again and again— however, his reinforcement was gone. Claire remained silent. Moving his eyes from the growing welts, Anthony noticed Claire's fist at her lips. He felt the red return with the realization that she was refusing to give him his satisfaction.

Crimson flooded the room. *Damn her!* She *would* learn that he was in control. She *would* learn to behave. She said she could follow directions—then by God, he had directions for her to follow. Reaching for her shoulder, he turned her over. Maintaining eye contact, Anthony began to undress. He didn't give instructions—at first. His intent was obvious.

With time, he began to direct her movements. His desired positions required her compliance and manipulation. Sometimes he told her what to do, other times he moved her as he saw fit. There were times he heard her ragged breaths or tasted her salty tears; nevertheless, Claire never argued nor told him to stop. *At least she seemed to comprehend their arrangement—this was consensual.*

By the time he finished, Claire seemed incapable of complete sentences. Her eyes no longer revealed her emotions; they were momentarily void and puffy and her cheeks were wet. Anthony refused to be affected by her demeanor. It reminded him of the woman he'd left two weeks ago in the suite and he didn't like it.

When he returned from the bathroom, Claire was still sitting on the floor holding her clothes. He walked toward her. Her disheveled appearance and vacant look disgusted him. More than anything, he wanted her out of his office. "You may go to your suite, clean yourself up, and get ready to demonstrate to me again your ability to follow directions." It was as if his words unlocked the invisible bonds that held her in place and allowed her to move. While she mechanically dressed, he did his best to ignore her occasional ragged breaths. Before she left, he callously added, "Do not leave your suite until I decide. Your pass to roam has been revoked."

When she reached for the door handle, Claire turned back toward Anthony. Her lips incapable of words, her eyes questioned. Only after he nodded did she open the door and walk away. He listened to her shoes on the marble corridor. Out of mere curiosity, he went to his computer and found the camera's view of the foyer. When Claire started to walk past the stairs toward the outside doors, Anthony shook his head and began walking toward the front of the house. He didn't need to hurry. There was no way that she could escape the grounds; nevertheless, he'd just told her to stay in her suite. Going outside was definitely forbidden. By the time he made it to the foyer, she was halfway up the stairs. Though he stood near the banister and watched, she never turned toward him.

Satisfied, he went back to his office and resumed his work. Although he had a lot to accomplish, every now and then he would utilize the cameras and look into her suite. He had difficulty hiding the anticipation as he saw her on the sofa, freshly showered and redressed. A grin emerged from time to time as she sat and obediently waited for him.

Anthony Rawlings did not fail. Catherine was wrong. He would teach Claire that there were consequences.

———————◆•◆•◆———————

LATER THAT NIGHT, Anthony tested Claire's reflexes as he rolled her hard nipple between his fingers. Their perspiration, combined with his recent oral assault, left the dark red nub slippery under his grasp. Though it appeared that she tried to anticipate his next move, her bristling and flinching indicated that she was unable. It wasn't as though she could see what he was doing; her eyes were completely covered by the satin material. He imagined the green that lay beneath. Brushing away long, damp strands of hair from her blindfolded face, his thumb traced her swollen lips. Anthony was mesmerized by their color. It was almost as if she were still wearing lipstick, though he knew that hours earlier it had been worn away. Nearing his mouth to her ear, his warm breath bathed her skin, as goose bumps proclaimed their presence over her arms and legs. Though she had spoken earlier in their training, more recently only sounds had been offered. Anthony whispered in his most seductive voice, "I'll be right back."

She nodded and turned away from his voice.

Pulling her chin toward him, he asked, "Claire, what have I said about verbal responses?"

"Yes," her words choked, "you'll be back."

Stroking her hair, his cheeks rose. "That's a good girl. You're learning."

He lifted himself from the side of her bed and walked toward the bookcase. With each step, his muscles pulled, tight and defined by their recent exertion. The constant vibration of his phone suggested that something of the utmost importance required his attention. As he reached for his phone, he contemplated the woman before him.

Truthfully, he didn't mind the break. After what had transpired earlier in the day in his office, he was prepared for this night to go on for a long time; besides, he was beginning to enjoy the role of teacher. With Claire's recent attitude adjustment, he must be doing well. Grinning ruthlessly toward his student, he watched as her legs twisted in a way as to try to conceal her exposed body. He could help her—lift a sheet and cover her; after all, with her hands bound to the headboard, she wasn't going to succeed alone—but he didn't. He liked the view. She had an attractive body. As his gaze reluctantly moved from the bed, he tapped the screen of his phone and words and icons appeared.

Instead of the urgent business on the screen, he recalled the beginning of this lesson. He wasn't sure if the satin scarves were necessary or purely an exhibition of his control. Either way, Anthony knew he wasn't going to tolerate her ridiculous fighting any longer. She would learn her place.

The afternoon must have been educational, because as he secured the satin around her wrists, she didn't argue or beg. He asked her, "Do you know why I'm doing this?"

At first, due to her tears, her response was difficult to understand.

He continued, "A few weeks ago, I had scratches on my arms. That's not going to happen again."

Her eyes, yet to be covered by the satin, opened wide. "I'm sorry, Anthony; I won't scratch, I promise."

"You won't, but you did. Behaviors have consequences. Can you remember that?"

"Yes."

"Repeat what I just said."

"Behaviors have consequences."

"So, whose fault is it that your hands are bound?"

Again, the waterworks. "Mine—it's my fault."

He stroked her hair. "That's right."

"This morning, I told you to be in my office by 10:30 AM. Did you do as you were told?"

Her shoulders shuddered with her response. "No."

"Say it... what is my number-one rule?"

Claire's words were separated by exaggerated gasps of air. With each deep breath, her exposed breasts trembled. "Your rule... is to... do as you say."

"Did you do that?"

"No, I didn't do as I was told. I'm so sorry—i-it won't happen again."

He looked deeply into her eyes just before covering them with the satin. "No, Claire, it will not." Securing the knot, careful to avoid her hair, he asked, "I'm going to tell you what to do right now. Will you follow my number-one rule?'

Her hands were now secured and her eyes were covered. He considered her ankles, but liked the possibilities available if he left them unbound.

"Y-yes," she replied.

"Yes, what?"

"Yes, Anthony, I'll do as you say."

The screen of his phone brought him back to present and told him that he had two voice mails and three text messages. He looked past Claire to the clock. It was almost 7:00 PM and they hadn't eaten. He checked the text messages first. One from his assistant, informing him of an important email she'd sent regarding an upcoming meeting. The next was a text message from Brent Simmons, head of Rawlings Industries' legal department and Anthony's closest friend. It, too, discussed the email.

Anthony could access the email in question from his phone, but perhaps both he and Claire could use a break. Besides, he may need to make a call or two if this truly was a big issue. Whatever was happening apparently had more than a few feathers ruffled. Looking toward the bed, he knew that calling from this room was too risky. *What if Claire decided to make a noise?* He walked over to the bed and leaned over her. As he neared, he watched her body grow still. Running his fingers slowly over her breasts and down her stomach, he said, "I have to make a few calls. I'm going to untie you."

First, he untied the scarf, exposing her green eyes. Her makeup from earlier had smeared, and large black streaks covered her cheeks; nevertheless, from the moment he'd removed the blindfold, her eyes were fixed on his. She was learning the importance of eye contact. That was the first step of Anthony's *one step at a time* training. He thought of the process as somewhat similar to what it must be like to break a wild horse. It took time and the correct balance of negative and positive reinforcement. Smiling, he continued, "When I untie your hands, are you going to behave?"

Her response was barely a whisper. "Yes."

"As much as I appreciate verbal responses, I like them better if I could actually hear them, and I'd like them if they had more elaboration. Yes, what?"

Her lips trembled as she replied, "Yes, Anthony, I'll behave."

While he untied her wrists, he spoke, "I want you to take another shower and dress in a negligee—something black and long. I assume you remember my rules regarding attire? There'll be nothing under that negligee." Not waiting for an answer, he ran his thumb under her eye to smear more of the mascara. "You'll also need to fix your makeup. Don't take too long. I'll be back soon." Though she was no longer bound to the headboard, her hands were together over her chest as Anthony continued to release her wrists from the length of material.

"You need to drink some water. I don't want you to dehydrate, but do not go to sleep—I have plans. We have a long evening ahead."

Claire didn't speak. Once her hands were free, she rubbed her wrists, and her gaze searched for the robe she'd left lying near the bed. When she started to reach for it, Anthony corrected her. "No. I want to see you."

He watched as she struggled with the decision to leave the robe and obey his command. Finally, she started to step away from the bed. As she did, Anthony noticed the ever so slight shake of her head and grasped her arm. She stilled where he held her. "What?" he asked. "Tell me why you shook your head."

Claire stuttered. "I-I didn't, or at least I don't think I did."

His grasp tightened. "Claire, you'll be honest with me at all times. I saw you shake your head. What were you thinking?"

She closed her eyes and more tears cascaded down her cheeks. When she opened them, she said, "I was thinking."

"Don't make me ask you to elaborate—again."

"I-I was thinking that this can't be real. It's some kind of nightmare. It can't really be happening to *me*."

Anthony let go of her arm and noticed the redness from his grasp. Claire's hand immediately went to the spot and massaged. Standing, he looked down at her. "Oh, my dear, it's real, and don't pretend that you hate it. I can tell when someone enjoys herself and you," he inclined his head and broadened his grin, taunting, "have enjoyed yourself more than once this evening." When her eyes started to look away, he lifted her chin. "Haven't you?"

"Please—I don't want any of this."

"That wasn't what I asked." He intensified his grasp. "I like my questions answered the first time. Do you understand?"

Her neck straightened. The sudden determination he saw in her expression surprised him as she replied, "I understand, and despite what you think you may have sensed, NO! I have not enjoyed myself."

Oh, there was fire yet to tame.

When he didn't release her chin, Claire's tone softened, "Now, may I please go take another shower?"

Amused by her candor, he replied, "First, my dear, I don't believe you; however, I believe that you believe you. Therefore, I'll allow this little bit of dishonesty to go unpunished. I recommend that you remember for future reference, I will not tolerate lying or deception. When it is discovered, you will be sorry. Second, expressing gratitude for positive consequences is not only appreciated, it's expected. So, Claire, what do you say when someone does something nice for you, like for example, untying your hands?"

He savored the moment as she comprehended his words. With her neck still straight, her words issued forth, saturated with a combination of rebellion and sarcasm. "Thank you, Anthony."

He released her chin. "Very good—do you remember my instructions?"

"Yes, I remember." She stayed still. When he didn't speak, she added, "I'll be waiting for you."

"Then you may go."

He watched appreciatively as she walked unclothed to the bathroom and closed the door. Yes, she would come around. It may be a slow and agonizing process, but he had all the time he wanted. After the bathroom door shut, he walked around the bed and pulled on his trousers. He, too, could use a shower. Momentarily, he considered joining Claire. The smile that emerged had more to do with her reaction than his actions. There would be plenty of time for that. He'd told her that he would leave and return, and he was curious to see if she'd follow his directions. If she didn't, there would be consequences.

As he exited the suite, he called the kitchen. "Have dinner sent to Claire's suite in an hour."

Chapter 2

The symphony—Late May 2010

(Consequences—Chapter 8)

**In nature there are neither rewards nor punishments;
there are consequences.**
—Robert Green Ingersoll

FROM THE SPEAKER on Anthony's desk, he listened to his assistant's voice, "Shelly is on line three."

Anthony's thoughts went from the spreadsheet on his screen to his publicist. "Patricia, put her through."

Immediately, he heard Shelly's concern. "Mr. Rawlings, Jennifer McAdams is in Italy on a photo shoot, and it's lasted longer than she planned."

"And you're telling me this because—"

"Because, sir, she's supposed to accompany you *this* evening to the Quad City Symphony at the Adler Theater."

Anthony ran his fingers through his hair. *Damn—he'd forgotten all about that, and he actually enjoyed Jenny's company, unlike many of the women he's been seen with over the years.* "Well, then I'll cancel."

"With all due respect, you can't. The theater will remain open because of your donation. They're planning on your attending, and there's a long list of guests coming to see you..."

Shelly rambled about the importance of his presence, as Anthony thought more about the outing. *Could this be an unplanned opportunity to test Claire outside the estate?* His grin emerged— *outside*. She'd just recently earned her way outside of the house. Truthfully, she'd been doing much better than he imagined, and *outside* would've happened much sooner, if only she'd *asked*. He shifted slightly in his large leather chair. Even the slightest thought of his complete control over her life had an effect on his body.

Shelly's voice brought him back to the subject at hand. The idea of a new test intrigued him. This would push her outside of her newly established comfort level. Besides, if she accompanied him and succeeded, she could earn more privileges. If she failed—well, they both knew what that could bring.

Shelly's voice quieted. Anthony waited for her to continue. When she didn't, he asked, "What was that?"

"Do you want me to call Julia?"

"No." Although, like Jenny, Julia too was a model, she was too high-maintenance for Anthony's liking.

"Do you plan to attend alone?"

Anthony wrestled with his thoughts. *If he took Claire out in public and she failed, wouldn't Davenport, Iowa, be a better testing ground, than say Chicago or New York?* He could manage damage control much better in his own backyard, and taking her out into the world would accomplish another goal. Anthony truly wasn't convinced Claire contemplated the magnitude of his power. Oh, she saw his wealth regarding the estate, and her behavior had steadily improved over the last two months; however, *did she really comprehend his reach? Did she truly understand that any attempts at escape could be quickly thwarted?* Taking her to an event where he's the man of honor would show her firsthand the depth and breadth of his power. Anthony made his decision: it was time. "I won't be attending alone."

"You realize if your assistant accompanies you to any more events the papers will start to speculate."

What? He hadn't even thought about taking Patricia. Yes, she'd accompanied him to a few events, but it was totally platonic and, at the time, an outing of convenience. "I can assure you that *speculating* would be all they could do. She's only accompanied me a few times, and they were all business-related. There's nothing to speculate about. I'll be taking someone else."

"Would you like to ask this lady, or would you like me to call her?"

He had to stifle the chuckle that rumbled in the back of his throat. *Ask?* He had no intentions of *asking* this person. This person didn't have a choice in the matter—or any matter. After the first few *glitches*, she seemed to have come to terms with this reality. This outing would be another duty she could fulfill. Anthony was growing tired of the parade of women on his arm. He had a lot of deals in the works, and listening to some woman prattle small talk didn't sound appealing. If he took Claire, he could avoid the whole wine-and-dine thing. They would simply attend the symphony and come home. It was much simpler.

"No, I don't need you to call."

"Mr. Rawlings, I'll need a name."

Of course she would. "Her name is Claire Nichols. She's from Atlanta."

Shelly didn't speak.

"Did you get that?"

"I did, sir. Is there more?"

"No. That's all that needs to be released."

"Perhaps you'd like me to do some research and verify that there isn't a history that could negatively affect you?"

"No." He sat taller. "There's no history. If that's all, I have work to do."

"Mr. Rawlings, can you please spell Nichols for me?"

Anthony gripped the receiver. "N-I-C-H-O-L-S." He tried to soften his tone. After all, Shelly was paid very well to maintain his reputation. He'd never before turned down her help in assuring its untarnished veneer. He explained, "I've already had her investigated." Sighing. "You know me, Shelly. I wouldn't take that risk; however, she's not the type of woman I normally see. The whole public thing is new to her. I don't want her getting unwanted publicity."

Shelly exhaled. "Yes, I can imagine that would be difficult. Very well, her name and hometown will be all the information that I release. Thank you, Mr. Rawlings. That's all I have at the moment."

"Very well." He hung up the receiver. *Shit! Was that the right call?* Rolling his mouse over the mouse pad, Anthony Rawlings' spreadsheets came back to life. A committee had worked days—perhaps weeks—compiling all the data; yet he wasn't seeing the numbers. No, he was seeing the woman back at the estate.

In the beginning, Anthony worked to make her a faceless person—perhaps like an employee at a business he was about to close. He told himself that she was nothing to him. Allowing Claire to pay her family's debt was not Nathaniel's original plan; however, Anthony reasoned, that some fates were worse than death. Catherine disagreed—at first—but she came around, and although he valued her opinion, Anthony's money propelled their plan. He'd do whatever he damn well wanted. He saw by the way Catherine pursed her lips and stared, that she wasn't pleased with his decision, but when it came to this matter Anthony wouldn't budge—Claire was different.

Truly, it was ironic that he'd made his case—*his* basis for *his* decision—based on the fact that she was *unique,* when he continually told himself she wasn't special. That was why he wanted to take her to the symphony—because she *wasn't* special. He wouldn't need to listen to her small talk, although he knew for a fact that Claire liked to talk! He wouldn't need to do anything that was expected on a *date.* Anthony could do whatever *he* wanted—this wasn't a date!

This outing would be a test. He squared his shoulders and dialed Catherine's cell number on his private cell phone. She answered after only a few rings. "Yes, Anton?" *Obviously, she was alone.* In the company of others, she maintained a more formal appearance.

"Have Claire ready by 6:00 PM. She's accompanying me to the symphony in Davenport."

"Excuse me?"

Anthony slowed his words. "Did I stutter?"

"I just think I misunderstood you. I'm not sure she's ready for this. Do you realize what could happen if—"

"Then make sure she's ready and that nothing happens. I'm not in this alone."

"I was not in favor—"

"But," he paused, "you've supported my decision. I believe the word is *accomplice.*"

Catherine's tone hardened. "I'll have her ready."

"Six PM, there's a cocktail reception at 7:00 PM, and the symphony begins at 8:00 PM. Eric will be driving us in the limousine."

"Anton, I'll prepare her, but you must be sure she—"

"Do you doubt my control?"

"No, that's not what I mean." Her tone changed. "Mr. Rawlings, she'll be ready."

He placed his cell phone back in his pocket and once again concentrated on the report before him.

———————◆———————

ANTHONY LOOKED AT his watch—5:52 PM—as he stood near the front door and replied to the text message that had just come across the screen of his iPhone. Eric was in front of the house with the limousine. Just as Anthony was about to hit *SEND*, he heard a cough from the top of the stairs. Looking up, he saw Catherine whisper something into Claire's ear, just before Claire began to descend. He scanned her figure from head to toe. Anthony liked her hair style. It was up, with curls hanging down, accentuating her slender neck. The dress she wore looked like it had been made especially for her petite frame. He also saw her heels peeking out from the bottom of her skirt with each step. She definitely looked the part—a far cry from the woman in jeans and tennis shoes at the Red Wing, the one he'd seen a few months ago.

He had a fleeting thought about Claire's public behavior; however, as he watched his acquisition gracefully approach, his concern evaporated into an aura that had enveloped the foyer. It felt nothing like the women who usually accompanied him. They had a confidence—no, arrogance—that surrounded them like a cloud of perfume. Claire's semblance was different. She had to know how beautiful she looked, yet he saw the question in her eyes. He'd seen it before. Claire wasn't contemplating her escape; she was seeking his approval.

A split second before his words of approval left his lips, he saw Catherine. After their discussion earlier, he questioned whether she would do her part to make this happen. Anthony turned from Claire and with a satisfied grin, bowed toward Catherine. "My dear Catherine, you've outdone yourself. You're an artist."

He saw the smirk in her eyes. Oh, if they were alone, he was sure Catherine would let him know exactly what she'd done to prepare Claire, not to mention what she thought of this outing; instead, she replied, "Mr. Rawlings, an artist is only as good as her canvas. You're accompanying a beautiful canvas."

"Or, should we say," he smirked, "she's accompanying me?" Turning back to Claire, he said, "We must go; Eric's waiting."

Claire didn't respond other than to nod. When Anthony offered his arm, she dutifully placed her small hand appropriately and walked with him to the limousine. Eric stood ready and opened their door. As they neared, Claire hesitated. *What was she thinking?* Many times her feelings were transparent; however, when he looked down at her, dressed, styled, and painted to perfection, he found it intriguing that he couldn't read her thoughts. Anthony motioned toward the open door, and once again, Claire nodded and eased herself inside.

After the car began moving, Anthony asked, "Have you ever ridden in a limousine before?" He knew the truth; she'd been in a limousine in Atlanta, as well as in Iowa. Anthony doubted she remembered either of those times—just as well.

"No, I haven't." She turned back toward him. "Anthony?"

Before she could continue, his phone vibrated. He held up a finger and she pressed her lips together. The call was from Tom, a friend as well as one of his legal staff. Before long, Anthony was in a full-out discussion about a company in Rhode Island. Thankfully, he could access some of the documents from his iPad. It wasn't until he sensed the car slow and turn, that he even realized how close they were or how much time had passed. If this had been a date, he never would have gotten so much accomplished. Smiling at his productivity, Anthony turned off his iPad, put his phone away, and turned toward Claire. "Has Catherine prepared your behavior for this evening as well as she has your appearance?"

Her eyes widened as she turned from the window to face him. "She's given me her advice," Claire answered. "But I'd feel better if I heard yours."

He liked her respectful tone. "Very well, when we arrive there'll probably be photographers. Don't act surprised or shocked by the attention. Just flash a beautiful smile and radiate confidence. Stay next to me at all times. There'll be reporters who'll try to learn your identity. I have a publicist who'll know the time to release any necessary information. That is *not* you. I'll do most of the talking; however, common sense will need to be with you. If spoken to, you will respond, but do *not* share information that is privileged. Do you understand?"

"I do."

"I've been asked to attend this event because of a donation I made to the Quad City Symphony and the Support the Arts Foundation. Have you ever been to a symphony before?"

"No."

"The symphony is a delightful evening. I believe you'll enjoy the music. This conductor is incredibly talented."

"Thank you, Anthony, for allowing me to join you this evening."

"I admit you've learned your lessons well. Now it's time to see if you can continue to follow the rules outside the boundaries of my estate."

"I'll do my best."

Anthony reached for Claire's chin, turned it toward him, and slowed his words. "You *will* succeed. Failure in a public setting is not an option."

He locked his eyes on hers and waited for an appropriate response. It didn't take long. "Yes, Anthony. I will continue to follow your rules."

"I assume you're currently following *all* of my rules?" He lifted a brow.

Claire nodded as her cheeks flushed.

"We can investigate that later," Anthony taunted as he placed his hand on her thigh.

When he moved his hand upward, she whispered, "I am."

He already knew the answer. First, she didn't own any panties, and as he helped her into the car, he'd allowed his hand to graze her firm behind. If there'd been anything under the beaded fabric, he would've known. He only mentioned his rule as a reminder of his authority. Anthony knew from Catherine that his forbiddance of undergarments continued to make Claire uncomfortable. He wanted Claire to remember as she interacted with strangers that he controlled everything. There was nothing he couldn't do to her, or make her do. Exposing her in public with absolutely nothing under her expensive dress reinforced his stance.

When the car slowed and stopped, Anthony whispered, "Wait for Eric. He'll open the door and assist you in getting out. I'll be right behind you, and we'll enter the theater together."

As he glanced out the limousine's window, Anthony realized that he'd underestimated the importance of this event. It may be only Davenport, Iowa, but the sidewalk was roped off and cluttered with reporters. If Claire chose to stand before them and make a public announcement about kidnapping, even he might not be able to manage damage control.

Although he was glad that he'd just reminded Claire of his rules, he worried if it had been enough. He didn't have time to discuss the consequences of failure. As soon as they were out of the car, Anthony put his hand in the small of her back and directed her away from the reporters. The contact served as her reminder—her warning. By the time they reached the second level and cocktails, people were coming from every direction.

It was as he handed Claire a glass of champagne that his anxiety began to wane. He saw in her eyes—those green eyes—her unfulfilled need for his approval. This time, he smiled and whispered in her ear, "You are truly lovely tonight." Instantaneously, he knew that Claire wouldn't disappoint him. She wouldn't escape or make a public announcement. It wasn't her words; she hadn't spoken. It was her countenance—he just knew. Each time he introduced her or she spoke, she impressed him with her performance. When the lights flashed, he guided her to their private box. It was a place where he'd sat many times—just a box; nonetheless, Claire scanned the auditorium like a child surveying the tree on Christmas morning.

He reminded himself that she hadn't seen anything, other than his estate, in over two months.

Before he could process her behavior and allow the relief of her compliance to truly settle in, the auditorium darkened, and the curator began to speak—it was about him. Suddenly, the spotlight hit their box, and Anthony did what he'd always done—appeared the perfect gentleman. The entire time he smiled and waved, he imagined the possibility of Claire jumping up and running for the hills. As he sat back down, her expression was unexpectedly pleasant. He leaned over and gently took her hand. Quite honestly, there wasn't anything he couldn't or hadn't taken from her. She belonged to him—all of her. They had a contract. He reached for her hand for one reason. It was an unspoken warning, just as when he touched the small of her back. The contact was his silent reminder to follow his rules.

When the last song ended and the conductor faced the crowd, Anthony looked toward his acquisition. The evening had gone even better than he imagined. His mind swirled with the possibilities of future events. It would be a relief to not have to deal with other women and their baggage. With this arrangement, he could do anything he wanted and, apparently, still be accompanied by the perfect companion. When Claire whispered her gratitude in his ear, Anthony knew she deserved something for her behavior—a positive consequence.

In the limousine, he watched as she fidgeted near the window. The confidence from the theater seemed to dissipate into the cool evening air. Before he could give it much more thought, she turned toward him. Her voice filled the quiet cabin. "That was a magnificent evening. Thank you, again."

Her sudden surge of straightforwardness caught him by surprise. "Do you really think so?"

"I do. The music was performed beautifully, and you were right about the conductor." After a pause, she asked, "Did I do all right?"

"What do you think?" he taunted.

After a moment, she replied, "I think I did well. I listened to Catherine, and to you, and d-did well."

It wasn't that he didn't enjoy the trepidation in her voice; however, if she were to accompany him on future outings, positive reinforcement was in order. He was prepared. Anthony reached into his briefcase and found the black velvet box. He didn't know that Claire would be accompanying him until this afternoon and didn't have time to buy anything; then he remembered the old necklace he'd found in her apartment. While he was home, he put it in his briefcase in anticipation of just such an occasion.

Extending the box toward her, he softened his tone. "I believe you did well. I've told you that every action has a consequence. That can be negative—as we've seen—or positive. I believe that tonight you earned a positive consequence."

"Anthony, I don't need a gift. I wanted to make you proud. If I did that, then I'm happy and that's enough."

"It's a gift, or at least I believe it was; however, it's not new." He continued to hold the box in her direction. Her tentative response caused his cheeks to rise. She was so unlike the other women he'd dated. Curiously, he asked, "Will it always be this difficult to get you to open gifts?"

She took the box. "You have my curiosity piqued. What are you giving me that's old?"

Before he could answer, she lifted the lid. When she looked up, tears silently glided down her cheeks. He'd seen her cry before—this was different. He listened as she choked back her emotion. "H-how did you... where did you get this? It was my grandmother's."

"It was in your apartment in Atlanta when it was cleaned out. I thought you might want to have it. Do you?" He watched as Claire internalized his words. In essence, he'd just told her that her old life was now cleaned out, disposed of—gone. She hadn't asked, and he hadn't informed her, but now it was confirmed. Anthony waited for her to respond.

"Oh, yes, I do!"

Her concentration on the necklace and acceptance of her apartment's fate satisfied him more than he'd expected. It confirmed that the *old* Claire Nichols was ceasing to exist, and with each passing day, the woman before him was new and created solely for his liking. His cheeks rose with the unexpected wave of relief. Eagerly, he asked, "Would you like me to help you put it on?"

Claire nodded and turned away as he draped the delicate chain around her neck. Past experience confirmed that the woman he initially acquired from Atlanta would've dwelled on her loss and become emotionally distraught. Claire's steadily improving behavior filled Anthony with pride. He'd done this! There wasn't a challenge that Anthony Rawlings couldn't overcome. Perhaps some of the credit should go to Catherine. Either way, he was enjoying the benefits of *their* dedication to their project.

As he fastened the clasp and the tips of his fingers touched her warm skin, Anthony remembered why he liked Claire's hair styled up. He leaned nearer to taste her exposed neck, but before his lips contacted her skin, she bent forward and pulled a small compact from her purse. A reprimand was on the tip of his tongue, when he realized that she hadn't moved away from him. She was still too wrapped up in the necklace to sense his intentions.

Her gaze flitted from the small mirror to him, as she said, "Anthony, there isn't a necklace you could've bought that would mean more to me than this one."

He'd seen many emotions in her emerald eyes, but what he saw at that moment gave him an unexplained sense of contentment. Anthony's thumb gently brushed her cheek, confirming that her tears from earlier were dry, unexpectedly her lids fluttered, and she moved toward his touch. Anthony knew that many times her words were false. He didn't consider it deception, but rather obedience. She said what she was expected to say and did what she was expected to do. There were also times when her expression failed to hide her trepidation, and he saw her true exposed reaction. This moment was different—real, not contrived—but honestly pleasant. He'd planned to give her the necklace as a reward, if she performed well; however, what he said next hadn't been planned. "People who know me well, and they're numbered, call me Tony. You may call me *Tony*."

"Thank you, *Tony*," she replied. "This has been an amazing night. How can I ever thank you?"

He pulled her close, feeling the pressure of her breasts against his chest. Turning off the riding lights, he smiled a devilish grin. "I have a few ideas."

Claire's glance darted toward the dark glass partition separating the back from the front of the car.

Tony laughed. "I promise we're alone; Eric can't see or hear us." He leaned toward her. She instinctively reached for his neck and settled onto the long leather seat. As he hovered mere inches above, he watched her cheeks flush, and his erection came to life. Over the past few months, Claire had learned to respond to Tony's commands—both verbal and otherwise. There'd been times when she'd hesitated. It was on those occasions that she earned the punishment she deserved. Turning his tone more serious, he raised a brow and demanded, "Now, show me that you've followed my rules. I want to see."

Claire's immediate response fortified the pride of his accomplishment. She maintained their gaze as her small hand fumbled for the hem of her dress. "I can't reach—"

Tony wouldn't let her finish—he couldn't. He needed to taste her. Entwining his fingers in her loose ringlets of hair, he tilted her lips upward and heard a small moan before his mouth seized hers. Unable to soften his approach, he took what was his. It wasn't enough—he wanted more. When his tongue probed, her lips parted, allowing him to enter her warmth. Tony savored her sweetness as her arms once again encircled his neck. With his other hand, he reached for the hem of her dress and the cabin filled with her whimpers of anticipation.

He slowly lifted the beaded material and teasingly brushed her inner thigh. "Open your legs for me," he commanded.

She obeyed and he continued to caress her soft skin. When her breathing labored and he neared his destination, Tony stopped. Releasing her hair, he sat up and gazed down at her blushed cheeks, smudged lipstick, and nearly exposed body. Grinning, he murmured, "You were amazing tonight."

Softly, she replied, "Thank you."

Taking her in, he reminded her. "But the night isn't over." His playful tone vanished. "Now, lift your dress and let me see if you have truly behaved."

Slowly reaching for the length of material, Claire kept her eyes fixed on his. As the material rose, she replied, "I promise, Tony. I've followed your rules."

He couldn't help but think how beautiful she looked—offering herself to him. That, combined with the sound of her calling him by his personal name, was enough to release the painful tightness in his slacks. It seemed unreal that he could be on the verge of exploding, and she'd yet to touch him. Surprisingly, at that moment, that wasn't what he wanted. He yearned for something else, and they both knew his desires came first.

Taking off his jacket and then his tie, Tony continued to devour Claire with his intensifying gaze. He couldn't look away as she silently watched his every move. When he slowly and deliberately moved to his knees and grinned, he sensed her relief. It intoxicated him that something as insignificant as a change in his facial expression could influence her world. Beckoned by her scent, his sultry tone returned. "Yes, I would say you have been a very good girl."

He lifted each one of her soft, smooth calves, savoring their shape while in the high heels, and rested them on his broad shoulders. With his intentions clear, Claire tipped her head back against the leather seat. Soon, her moans from earlier returned and grew louder. When her fingers gripped the leather seat, and he knew that she was about there, he stopped. It was his private game, but she was learning the rules.

"Tell me," he commanded.

"Anth—Tony, please."

"Tell me who you belong to."

"You, I belong to you." She fidgeted against the leather.

"Because," he prompted.

"You own me."

"Until?" He taunted her, teasing, kissing, and suckling her inner thigh.

"Please!" She took in a deep breath. "Until you decide."

"Say it."

"You own me until you decide."

"Good girl. Perhaps—" he reached for her skirt, bunched around her waist.

"Please," she begged, holding tightly to the material. "Please, don't stop."

Grinning and satisfied, Tony resumed his quest. Oh, there were times he'd leave her like this—unsatisfied—and make her switch places. It would be then that she would fulfill her duty. Of course, she didn't have the option to stop or taunt. Other times, he'd take the conversation further, making her tell him the amount of money he'd spent to secure her financial freedom.

Not tonight. Tonight Tony wanted to experience the benefits of her positive consequence. It didn't take long before he did.

Chapter 3

Passing and failing, both have Consequences
—July 2010

(Consequences—Chapter 9)

———————◆———————

Failure is no more a permanent condition than success! For
even if you succeed, there's still another test.
—Gene Bedley

As Eric approached the house, Tony took in the dark windows and glanced at the corner of his iPhone—after 10:00 PM. Since Claire's windows faced toward the backyard and woods, he couldn't see them or her balcony. He could imagine them and her suite... and her in her suite, with no other purpose than to wait for him. It was a thought that seemed to be recurring more and more often, slipping unexpectedly into his consciousness. *Why not?* She was in his house solely for his pleasure and enjoyment, and after the day and evening he'd just had, he deserved some *him* time.

After three months, he admitted—at least to himself—that this arrangement was working better than he ever predicted. Each test he presented, or that presented itself, solidified his control and power over Claire's life. He controlled everything about her—almost. Tony had allowed Catherine to share in his power, to a point. He set boundaries and Catherine adhered to them. She couldn't overturn any of his decisions. Tony didn't want Claire to think she could pit one of them against the other. Besides, Catherine's reign dealt with mundane day-to-day issues—clothing and schedules. Tony controlled the more important matters, and of course, if he decided to trump Catherine's plans for a day, he did.

That would happen on days that Tony decided to work from home. He'd made it clear that when he was home, Claire was to be available to him at all times. On those days, he'd not only trump Catherine's plans, but Claire's too.

From the first time he'd allowed Claire access to the grounds of the estate, Tony saw how much she enjoyed that little liberty. Without saying it, she savored those outings as her own personal escape. The fact that she willingly and of her own accord returned to the house at her appointed time, appeased his sense of control, enticing him to allow that privilege to continue.

Each morning Claire followed a routine that included swimming and weights. Tony enjoyed the benefits of her workout and had no desire to stop that activity; however, by 10:00 AM on the days that he worked from home, her plans no longer mattered. She was expected to be in his office. Sometimes he'd acknowledge her presence; other times he'd be preoccupied. It didn't matter. On those days, her time, her schedule, and her body were at his disposal. He found it as intoxicating to make her sit and waste her day as it was to use her services. One of the best aphrodisiacs he knew was looking up from his computer or watching during a telephone call as Claire looked longingly out the window. Hell—he'd even find himself imagining that scene while in his corporate office.

As he walked through the dimly lit hallway toward his office, his anticipation grew. The day had been long. There was no better word. It wasn't bad or upsetting; it wasn't good or rewarding—it was *long*. Not only were there multiple big deals and negotiations in the works, Tony had to spend the evening at a dinner meeting that turned into a few drinks and more negotiations. Public outings weren't his thing.

Fundraisers and social functions that could double as tests were increasingly more fun. Being a multi-tasker extraordinaire, Tony could shake hands, carry on a conversation, and monitor Claire's every move. That said, his preferred evening destination was more intimate, and lately had become even more inviting. At the end of a long day, he wanted to be behind the iron gates of his estate.

Inside the top side drawer of his desk, Tony found Claire's driver's license. For a long time it had been stashed away with other items from her apartment, but just like her grandmother's necklace, it was time to present Claire with a new gift. A grin came to his lips as he considered the small card; it would have a companion, or should he say, a tool for a test. The companion card arrived to his office earlier in the week. It was an *American Express* platinum card with Claire's name embossed upon the front. He planned to tell her that it was her reward for her recent public behavior—that wouldn't be a total fabrication. The way she handled the reporter recently was stellar; she'd been presented with an opportunity to reveal her true status and chose instead to abide by his rules. Nonetheless, providing her limited access to a credit card and her driver's license had other benefits. Over the last two months, she'd been seen with him on multiple occasions; he needed a cover story. If she ever attempted to reveal the truth, he needed something to make her accusations seem implausible. *What better cover than his money?* He'd taken away her debt—he could prove that. With her new credit card, she wouldn't only be seen as his *companion*, but as a woman spending *his* money. No one would believe that she wasn't enjoying his fortune of her own free will.

When he first brought Claire to Iowa, he wasn't sure how involved the plan would become. Each day presented additional choices and decisions. Thus far, in his opinion, Tony had developed the perfect plan—one that continued to weave fresh possibilities. As each new thread was revealed and sewn into place, Tony's omnipotence grew. There wasn't an angle he hadn't considered.

He placed her driver's license and the credit card into a small, feminine leather wallet, flung his jacket on the desk chair, and headed toward Claire's suite. The summer heat was sweltering, and the loss of one layer of clothing felt liberating as he briskly walked up the backstairs. Mindlessly, he imagined that in a very short time he'd be losing more layers. It was a scenario that had been playing in his head over and over throughout the god-awful dinner meeting. Grinning, he wondered if that was what had kept him from going off and telling his dinner guests what he really thought of their ideas.

Often, when he first got home, Tony would go to his suite or office and relax before joining Claire. On those days, he turned on the feed to her suite and watched as she prepared for his arrival. Tonight, it was too late for him to check the video feed, and honestly, he was too anxious to use her and forget his long day. It didn't matter. Her behavior had become reassuringly predictable.

In stunned disbelief, Tony opened Claire's door to an empty suite. He walked to the closet/dressing room and then to the bathroom. With each unoccupied space, his sense of gratitude for her recent obedience swiftly morphed into a combination of alert and anger. *Where the hell was she? Why wasn't she where she was supposed to be?*

Throwing the wallet—the reward he'd meant to present to her— onto her table, he stormed out of her suite. When he reached the bottom of the stairs, he called out for Catherine. She'd better damn well know Claire's whereabouts. As he turned the corner, the glow of the pool's colored lights illuminated the windows at the back of the sunporch. The movement of the water caught his attention. He'd found Claire.

He stood unseen within the darkened room and watched her every move. It was like his hidden cameras, but somehow more intimate. Claire moved slowly, floating on her back and staring up to the sky. It wasn't that he gave his acquisition much thought; however, there were times that it amazed him that Claire could find pleasure in the most mundane of activities.

As he watched, his thoughts of anger and betrayal returned. She was outside enjoying a swim, when she was supposed to be available to him! She had the whole damn day to do whatever she wanted. Disappointment and fury overcame him. Perhaps he was wrong to present her with a new freedom. After all, he'd thought they were past reinforcing the most basic of his rules.

Cloaked in the shadow of the night, he stepped from the house and approached the pool. Within seconds his linen shirt dampened and clung to his back. Each step away from the air conditioning reminded him of the oppressive summer heat. Even in the darkness, he felt the heat of the day's intense sun roll off the concrete deck. His voice boomed over the hum of the pool's filter and the distant call of country crickets. "Claire, what in the hell are you doing?"

She didn't move as she blissfully floated, staring upward. Momentarily, Tony followed her gaze. It was a sky and there were stars. He saw no reason for her to give it her full attention. "Claire, get out of the damn water!"

Each insubordination added fuel to his nearly combustible disposition. Walking out of the shadows to the edge of the pool, he saw how the brightly illuminated water ebbed and flowed over Claire's flat stomach and her bathing-suit-clad breasts moved with her steady breathing. Her hair floated in a halo around her face, and the streaks of blonde that infiltrated her chestnut hair reflected the fountain's colorful display. She wasn't watching the stars: her eyes were closed. His volume decreased, but his tone remained determined. "Claire, you know better. You know my rules. You're supposed to be in your suite."

It was then her eyes sprang wide and she righted herself, beginning to tread water and twist her head from side to side. "Tony, you startled me. Catherine said you wouldn't be home until late."

He stared at her for a moment, waiting—he wasn't sure for what, perhaps an apology, perhaps an explanation. She continued to tread water as she looked up at him with her damn green eyes. It wasn't his plan for the evening, but as the perspiration dripped from his shoulder blades to the middle of his back, Tony knew what he wanted.

Without speaking, he stepped back into the darkness and ridded himself of his encumbering clothing. With each article removed, he felt the weight of the day lift, as oppression transformed into a newfound source of energy. His goal for the night—his chosen activity—hadn't changed. Tony knew what he wanted, and without question, it would be his. The destination of his conquest was truly insignificant, and besides, the water looked increasingly inviting. Moments later he dove into the colorful liquid and seized the object of his quest.

He didn't need to ask permission or engage in customary expected conversation. She was his for the taking. When he surfaced mere inches away, he wrapped his arms around her body, and Claire gasped. Her soft, cool skin did nothing to cool his desire. Turning her to face him, his mouth emphasized his claim while his skillful fingers removed the top of her bathing suit. A simple pull of two strings and her round supple breasts were his for the taking.

The pressures of the day and the disappointment of her empty suite erupted in a force of energy he had no wish to control. As her hard nipples pressed against his chest and their tongues united, his anger waned. The fury that had been building found a new outlet. Walking toward the deep end of the pool, he tugged at the strings on the side of her bathing suit bottom and it too floated to the depths.

Lifting Claire momentarily away, his eyes scanned up and down her newly exposed flesh. Dutifully, her gaze met his. Releasing his hold, her small hands reached for his shoulders. It may have been due to the depth of the water, but that was not what Tony chose to believe. In his mind, it was her silent way of accepting what he had to offer. As she wrapped her legs around his torso, he fought the urge to take her right then. He could do whatever he desired, but rushing was not his plan.

When his mouth once again found her breasts, his teeth nipped at the hard nubs, and his fingers explored and caressed. Her wordless moans encouraged, and despite the coolness of the water, when Claire's back arched, allowing him better access, his body responded.

No longer was he thinking about his day at work or his dinner meeting. Even memories of Claire's empty suite were lost to their new world. No one else existed within their colorful abyss. He nipped and taunted, cheered on by Claire's wordless sounds. He watched as her beautiful body stiffened and convulsed within his hold. By the time she fell slack against his shoulder, tried to steady her breathing, and held tightly to his neck, Tony knew what he wanted next. Carrying her to the steps, he helped her from the pool. She took his hand and followed him on wobbly legs to one of the large cushioned lounge chairs hidden in the shadows. Even in the darkness, he watched as her eyes fluttered and her body accepted him without question. He didn't need to verbally direct her movements. A simple touch and she responded to his desire.

With their bodies damp and their breath resuming normal inhales and exhales, Tony grinned. He watched the clouds of uncertainty dissipate from her emerald eyes as they glistened with the reflection of the pool's fountains. "Good evening, Claire." Her responding smile quickly faded when he added, "I wasn't happy when you weren't in your suite." He touched her lips, stopping whatever it was that she was about to say, and continued, "But your idea of a swim on this hot evening was much better than what I had planned." As the words left his lips, Tony felt her body relax and watched her smile return.

Allowing his own grin to emerge, Tony asked, "Maybe we should go back into the water to cool off again?"

"That sounds nice," she agreed, as she willingly placed her small hand in his, and followed him back into the pool.

By the time they'd returned to Claire's suite and showered, Tony remembered his gift. The sight of her walking toward her side of the bed, wrapped in only a black silk robe almost pushed the conversation from his thoughts; however, he was interested in her reaction. He recognized that the best weapon in his arsenal that had worked to keep her compliant was her seclusion. Even with the vast expanse of his estate, she had limited personal interaction. Tony wasn't sure if she had truly accepted her fate, or if she were just so lonely that she would settle for his presence. Either way, it was obvious that Claire craved interaction. Whenever he presented the opportunity, she could talk for hours. Sometimes she spoke about her family or her previous life, but mostly it was about books or movies or nothing at all. During those times, it was as if a day's or a week's worth of conversation had been backlogged and suddenly released. He didn't mind. Actually, Tony learned a lot about Claire Nichols during those times.

As Claire was about to untie her robe, Tony pulled back the covers and patted the bed at his side. On most nights, Claire would lie down and silently wait for him to come to her. Her eyes darted to his, searching for the reason for his invitation. He smiled in response.

When she secured the silk, sat on the bed, and turned toward him, he purposely lowered his brow and shook his head. "No, Claire, the robe needs to go." With as many times as he'd seen her nude, it amazed him that she still held an air of modesty. He liked to push her to the edge of her comfort zone. Oh, who was he kidding? He liked to take her *out* of that zone. Watching her silent battle of wills, as she fought with what he told her to do and what she wanted or felt was proper, was addicting. He could do it all day.

After removing the robe, she worked her way across the expanse of the large mattress. He reached out and brushed a damp lock of hair from her face. Even without makeup, her eyes were stunning. They spoke to him in ways her lips would not. He knew her question before she asked; nevertheless, he waited for her to speak. "Why do you want me over here?" He enjoyed her directness. God knew, his request could be anything.

"I wanted to talk."

Her eyes lit as if someone had hit a switch. "Really?"

He smiled as he motioned for her to sit next to him. With her tucked against his shoulder, he allowed his fingertips to caress the softness of her shoulder.

Finally, she asked, "What do you want to talk about?"

"Your behavior." Her muscles went rigid. Tony lowered his tenor and commanded, "Claire, look at me." Her eyes slowly moved to his. Grinning at her obvious trepidation, he reassured. "Your behavior has been very good, and I believe you deserve a reward."

"Tony, I—"

"I'm specifically referencing the University of Iowa's Children's Hospital event."

Claire exhaled, her tension dissipated, and her body molded against the pillow. Tony marveled at how her warm, small frame fit perfectly under the crook of his arm. As she spoke, the sound of relief filled her voice. It seemed that as of late, she'd learned to control her words, especially when she was apprehensive or concerned; however, when she was comfortable, she spoke more freely. Surprisingly, he found that equally as rewarding. After all, with whom else did she have to talk? It was another of her needs that only he could fill. She rambled on. "I was so afraid. I was afraid that he'd get me to say something or misinterpret something that I said. I didn't want to interrupt you, but I didn't know what else to do. I—"

Shifting, she stopped talking and he felt the sensation of her warmth as their skin united. Nearing his lips toward hers, he reassured, "That was perfect." Softness filled the emerald shining back at him. Though his tone was soft, a certain part of his body was becoming painfully hard. "I have rules, Claire. Sometimes I need to be assured of your dedication to your job. To do that, I've presented you with tests, and there will be more in the future. Sometimes you'll pass those tests; sometimes you won't. What happens if you don't?"

"There will be consequences."

He grinned. "And what happens if you pass?"

Her expression brightened. "There will be consequences—good ones."

"Very good." His fingertips slowly traced an invisible track from her ear, down her neck, over her shoulder, down the curve of her breast, to her stomach, and back up the other side. With each pass, the track dipped lower and lower. A hint of sultriness entered his authoritative tone. "When we're out in public, your behavior is a reflection of me. How do I feel about public failure?"

Her hips lifted toward his touch, yet she obediently responded. "You... don't like it."

"I don't." He nibbled her neck. "If that would happen, I'd be disappointed." He reached for her chin. "Claire, do you want to disappoint me?"

"No..." Her legs opened, accommodating, allowing, and inviting his actions.

Tony couldn't continue this conversation much longer. "Open your eyes." She obeyed. "You should know, that reporter wasn't a planned test." She nodded. "But if it had been, you would have passed. That's why I believe you've earned the right to have more responsibilities and independence." He had her full attention. "On your table is a wallet. Inside that wallet you'll find your driver's license and a credit card. They're for you to use when I'm not around."

The sudden shock at his gift was evident. "What do you mean, when you aren't around?"

He chuckled. "No, Claire, I'm not setting you free; you have more debt to pay and you need my guidance. You've learned so much in this short time, and you have much more to learn. You won't leave the grounds alone. If you aren't with me, you'll be with Eric, and even then, it'll only be with my permission, but I need to travel to Europe for at least a week next month." He grinned. "You've behaved well." The track he'd been tracing suddenly extended over her buttocks and thigh. "Very well, and you've followed my instructions much better than I would've given you credit for a few months ago." His hands roamed. Claire's eyes closed and she willingly responded to his slightest inclination. "As a matter of fact..." His tone became playful. "...I believe that right now you would do as I say."

Her lids opened, veiling her eyes with her lashes. "I would," she purred.

Tony wondered if Claire knew how totally erotic her accommodating tone was to him. Was it real, or was she performing for her job? He didn't know. He did know that he had needs and desires, and if she was in this accommodating of a mood, the instructions were on the tip of his tongue. Grinning, he said, "I think we should continue to test that theory, but first, I believe you've earned the ability to do some shopping for yourself."

For a moment she seemed lost in thought.

"Claire?" Her gaze focused. "Let's see how well you can do with instructions tonight."

Chapter 4

Shall we go to the movies? —August 2010

(Consequences—Chapter 11)

———◆———

Everyone can be manipulated.
It's most successful by people who're closest to you.
—Aleatha Romig, Convicted

TONY LOOKED UP from his tablet and peered toward Claire as the car in which they rode wound around the twists and turns of the country roads near his estate. She was staring out the window, quieter than normal. Tony figured that the reason was his preoccupation with his work. Since they'd touched down from New York, he'd been busy with the onslaught of emails, and she knew better than to interrupt him when he was working. Sneaking another glance, he tried unsuccessfully to read her thoughts or decipher her mood. It was something that he didn't particularly like; he owned her—all of her, including her thoughts. Most of the time, his acquisition was an open book. The fact that she could, at times, successfully hide or mask her true emotions irritated him. Usually, he could look at her and intuitively know exactly what she wanted or needed. Her eyes were the key. Sometimes they held a fire of confrontation even when her lips spoke obediently. It was quite the sight to witness, her battling with herself. Tony found her internal struggle very entertaining; however, what he currently witnessed was a newer phenomenon. Claire's expression, including her eyes, was of complete contentment—no, perhaps, indifference. There was something about her body language that didn't match.

Maybe he'd pushed too far during his celebration yesterday? He remembered going back to his New York apartment and finding her asleep on his bed. He hadn't intended for the afternoon and evening to go as it had, but one thing led to another. Besides, it didn't matter. He had the right to push as hard and as far as he wanted. Claire had a job to do, a role to play, and her satisfaction with her job was inconsequential. She would do what was required of her, or she'd face the consequences. Perhaps that was what she was thinking about as they approached his estate—how her life was truly out of her hands, in every way. Oh, if only he could confirm that. It would please him to no end, to know that she had finally succumbed completely to his obvious authority.

Exhaling, he realized he'd lost interest in the information on the screen of his iPad. Closing his eyes, he defined the woman next to him. She was his acquisition, *his prisoner*—a sacrificial lamb for the sins of her forefathers. She was his; he needn't concern himself with worries over her emotional well-being. After all, her physical needs were more than being met. He'd spent a fortune to rid her of debt. She lived on a multi-million-dollar estate, and her clothes, as well as food, were amply supplied. She also had an active sex life. While pleasing her wasn't his top concern, she obviously enjoyed herself quite a bit of the time.

Tony worked to push his thoughts away. He had a lot to accomplish before he left for Europe, and truly, Claire Nichols' happiness, or lack thereof, needn't clutter his radar. As they neared the estate, he remembered his last conversation with Catherine. He knew that she didn't mean her comments the other morning. After all, she'd apologized for them. Glancing again at Claire, he questioned if his behavior yesterday afternoon and night was incited by that conversation. He tried to deny it, but Catherine's concerns ate at him. Even now he was thinking about that conversation:

At a little after 3:30 AM, there was no need for formalities. Catherine didn't knock or address him with any sort of conventionality as she opened the door to his office, secured her bathrobe, and began speaking, "Just because you can't sleep, doesn't mean that I don't. Tell me why on earth you summoned me here at this ungodly hour. Besides, don't you need to leave for New York this morning?"

"Good morning, to you, too. I will be leaving in a few hours, and I woke you because I'm taking Claire. You need to pack her things."

Catherine shook her head. "You're what? Have you lost your mind?"

"I'm taking Claire with me to New York, and I believe that perhaps it's you who's delusional. This early hour has taken your candidness to the extreme. Do you have a problem with my decision?"

Catherine sat on one of the chairs by his desk and shook her head from side to side. "First, you start sleeping in her suite. Then, you take her out on public appearances. Now, you're going to take her to New York? They're already speculating about the two of you in the press. Are you trying to put her in the spotlight?"

Tony shrugged his shoulders as a faint grin emerged.

Catherine cocked a brow. "Explain yourself. Tell me, are you falling for her?"

"No. How about you? Is she fulfilling some unmet motherly need?"

Catherine suddenly stood and the chair where she'd been sitting pushed against the wall. Her gray eyes glared in response. "Anton, that isn't even possible. You know I don't want to discuss that."

"Fine," he agreed. "I won't make assumptions about your motives, if you don't make assumptions about mine."

"My motives. My motives!" Her volume increased. "I'll tell you my motives. They're to keep the two of us out of jail. I mean, seriously, if you'd stayed with the plan, the one we've had for a long time—if you'd stuck to that, there would be no witnesses, no connections, and we'd be safe. This—" she waved her hands toward the ceiling, "—was not our plan, and now you want to make her even more publicly visible?"

"My dear Catherine Marie..." he said, using her middle name was his way of calming her. She no longer used the name Marie, yet it reminded them both of his grandfather and, therefore, usually helped to soothe her temper. "...it's all about appearances. I'll admit that I've been spending most of my nights in her bed." He leaned forward. "If you were in my shoes, or out of them, I believe you'd do the same. It has more benefits than sleeping alone. Besides, technically, it's my bed, in my house, on my estate, and I can sleep anywhere I damn well please."

"I believe you're putting too much emphasis on those benefits. They're affecting your thinking."

He chuckled. "You see, that's where you're wrong. I know exactly what I'm doing. I've taken her out in public. She's been seen with me. While we're in New York, I've told her that she'll shop."

Catherine resumed her seat. "Shop? So you want her to be visible?" She sat for a moment and contemplated. "Do you believe she'll be noticed? I'm not sure that the press will recognize her. Not without you, I mean."

"Maybe not, but Eric will. He'll get pictures." Tony's grin grew. "I consider it part of our insurance policy."

"She'll need to spend more money than she did last time. If you want to convince the world she's after your money, she'll need to buy more than a few blouses and a book."

"I'll emphasize that in my directive." He leaned back. "Faith, Marie, have faith."

"All right, since you've already put her out there, the more insurance the better. I just think it would've been better to not have had her out in public with you in the first place." She stood and walked toward the door. "I think it would've been better to stick with the original plan."

"She's not on a vacation," Tony reminded in a low, yet direct tone.

"Really?" Catherine turned toward him. "She dresses in the best clothing, she doesn't lift a finger, and now she's traveling. So she's satisfying your needs. I don't think she hates that—anymore."

He smirked. "Are you surprised? For your information, I could provide a long list of references who... don't hate it."

"Do I really care? No, I don't. I'm concerned."

"That?"

"That you're letting down your guard. I mean, who's really in control? How much is you, and how much is her manipulating you? You're a man. Men... well, men forget sometimes what part of their body should do the thinking." She softened her tone. "Anton, I don't want you to be swayed."

As Catherine went on about her concern, Tony remembered the night before in Claire's suite. It was the first time she'd willingly offered herself to him—and he allowed it. He didn't direct her movements or give instructions. He'd allowed her to seduce him, and now he's taking her to New York. Could Catherine be right?

When Catherine quieted, Tony replied, sounding more confident than he truly felt. "That's ridiculous. I didn't wake you for a debate. I woke you so that you could do what you do, and have her ready to board my plane by 6:00 AM. Do you think you can do that? Do you *think you can do your part of this project?"*

"Yes." Her neck stiffened. "I can do that." She rubbed her hands over the softness of her robe. "I'm sorry. You're right. I'm sure Claire Nichols isn't manipulating you. You're in much more control than that. I know you wouldn't want to disappoint Nathaniel that way. Besides, it sounds like this public appearance thing is well planned and thought out."

Tony nodded as Catherine disappeared around the partially open door.

So what? He liked sleeping in Claire's bed? That wasn't Claire's manipulation; it was *his* domination. He could wake her at any hour and expect complete compliance. Those were his thoughts as they passed through his gates and he placed his tablet in his briefcase. Moments later Claire's words refocused his attention.

"Tony, you said you built your house about fifteen years ago?"

"Yes, why do you ask?"

She continued to gaze toward the house. "I'm not used to seeing it from the front—it's beautiful."

"Thank you." He looked out the window as Eric stopped the car. It *was* a beautiful structure, an architectural wonder.

Claire continued, "But it looks older than fifteen years to me—the style I mean."

He nodded. "I patterned it after my family's home from when I was a child." His thoughts went to Nathaniel. *He wasn't disappointing him; this house was a testament to that.*

As they both exited the car, Claire's eyes widened with wonder. It was as if she were seeing the house for the first time, not as if she'd been living there for months. "I thought you built your fortune from nothing. How did your parents have a house like this?"

He looked at the combination of rock and stone—memories of an earlier time threatened to come forward. He pushed them away. "It was my grandfather's, not my parents. My father was weak. However, my grandfather's house and money were all lost over twenty-five years ago. My grandfather trusted the wrong people." Tony wasn't sure what propelled him to share that bit of information. He'd blame it on his recent thoughts of Nathaniel. No matter, it was true, and there was no way Claire would know her connection—but he did. Walking toward his office, Claire followed a few steps behind. Her sudden acknowledgement of the place wherein she'd been living for so long was amusing.

"It truly is amazing," she said. "Did you pattern the inside after it, as well?"

He shrugged. "Mostly. I even found and purchased some of the original artwork and antiques; however, I wanted my home equipped with all the modern conveniences and security equipment. Every inch of this house is under constant surveillance. I won't make the same mistake my grandfather made." Tony looked up from his desk to a bewildered expression. Suddenly, her placid veneer was gone. The wheels of understanding were visibly turning in her head. Tony continued, "Haven't you ever wondered how the staff knows exactly when to enter your suite?"

Her voice quivered, "Y-you mean *my suite* is under surveillance? L-like there are cameras?"

Revulsion emanated from her pained expression. When their eyes met, his grin widened. "Yes, of course. It's all video-recorded and saved." Claire visibly paled as she backed toward the wall and sat on the nearest chair. Basking in her newfound discomfort, Tony added, "Perhaps we could have a premiere viewing and critique? Then we could work on revisions."

"Tony, please tell me you're joking, some sort of *sick* joke."

He felt his power and control return. It was as if he'd just received a transfusion of domination. Yes, yesterday and last night he'd taken her body, but he'd done that before. This was so much more—her mind and her spirit. This was what she'd successfully kept from him. He stood taller with the revelation: it was now his for the taking, or it soon would be.

"But, my dear Claire," he cooed with mock adoration, "I am *not*. Now, the staff doesn't have access to the view of your bed—only I have that. They do have a view of the sitting area and the doorways to and from your dressing room and bath. That's how they've been able to come and go without your seeing them."

Her eyes filled with tears as she asked, "But why? Why would you do that? Why would you keep it?"

"Because I can—I can watch and decide what I like and what I believe can be improved. You'll understand after you get a chance to view it. Maybe tonight, but now I must be going." As Tony started to walk toward the hall doors, Claire sat statuesque. He reiterated, "It's time to exit my office." When she still didn't move, he casually added, "and in case you're wondering, yes, this room, too, is under surveillance—except for my desk. I do have a great view of the sofa and this open area." He gestured toward the place where he'd administered her first lesson in *actions and consequences*.

While her sudden look of desperation inspired him, he needed to go into Iowa City. The work at his corporate office wouldn't wait. "Claire, I need to go. Get out of the chair now."

Apparently, she was still capable of obeying, as she silently walked past him toward the stairs. Closing the door to his office, he smirked. *Who's manipulating whom?* He couldn't wait for the viewing.

As TONY WENT about his business at his corporate office, his mind continually looped back to his video library—there were so many. Between phone calls, spreadsheets, and meetings, he debated about which would be best to show Claire. He knew that she didn't want to see them—or star in them—or acknowledge them. It was obvious by her reaction. Until she responded so vehemently, he had no idea she'd detest the idea that much, but once she did, he knew he'd found that missing piece of the puzzle. That made the viewing all that much more special. Now, as he departed for ten days in Europe, he could leave confident, knowing without a doubt that he was in control.

——◆——

IT WAS TONY'S idea to eat on the patio. He called Catherine from the car and told her to have dinner served outside. He wanted the distractions of the outdoors. He hadn't been this excited about his plans for Claire in a while. That wasn't to say he didn't enjoy all of the uses he'd invented for her, but this was new. Concentrating on eating dinner in her suite or in the dining room with only the two of them would've been too difficult. The outdoor setting worked as a distraction—for him. Claire seemed to be another story. She wasn't her normal chatty self. She looked the part, dressed appropriately for dinner, nodded and responded at all the right times as Tony talked about New York, her shopping, his meetings, and his impending European trip, but her mind was obviously elsewhere. As much as he wanted to broach the subject of their movie night, he didn't, partially out of curiosity. He wondered if she would bring it up. There were times when she surprised him by jumping headfirst into conversations he was confident that she'd rather avoid. That candor and resilience amazed him. Tonight was different; Claire emanated an aura of defeat before the battle even began. No, he wouldn't bring it up; it was too enjoyable watching Claire push her food around her plate and sip her iced tea.

Perhaps, he pondered, she hoped that by avoiding the subject it would go away. That would not happen! His anticipation was palpable.

"You haven't eaten much of your dinner," Tony assessed.

She shook her head. "I guess I'm not hungry. I think traveling wore me out. I believe I just need to get some sleep."

He smirked. "You napped today."

Her eyes widened as they immediately looked to him. He loved the mixture of emotions that he witnessed flashing before him. Behind the green, he saw the realization that she'd just been caught in her attempt to sway the course of the evening. As a bonus, she also received confirmation of his ability to visually intrude into all aspects of her life. In all actuality, it had been Catherine who'd told him she'd napped, yet if Claire thought it was another example of his omnipresent power, who was he to dissuade her?

Softly, she replied, "Yes, I did; however, I'm not feeling well."

He grinned as he pushed back his chair and extended his hand. "Then, my dear, let's leave dinner behind."

Her eyes lightened as she placed her hand in his and stood. "Thank you."

"Oh, there's no need to thank me. I do, however, find it interesting that after all of these months, you believe you have the power to manipulate me and alter my plans."

"I don't know what you mean," she said, peering at him through her lashes.

When they walked through the sunporch and into the house, Claire turned toward the foyer. Tony's touch redirected her movements. "No, my dear, we aren't going upstairs." She inhaled and looked down. Tony lifted her chin. "I am a man of my word. I promised you something special tonight, and I fully intend to deliver."

"Tony, please... I-I'm really not feeling well. I think it was the trip. It was great to go someplace, but I'm not used to being away from here.

I'm sure I'll feel better tomorrow."

"But you see," he mocked, "I won't be here tomorrow, so our movie night can't wait."

He felt her tremble as they changed direction and headed for the lower level. "Are you cold?"

She shook her head and took a ragged breath. "N-no, I don't want to do this."

As they walked down the stairs, he pulled her close. When his lips grazed her ear, her neck stiffened. Seductively, he whispered, "You've said that before. Has it ever stopped my plans?"

Her shoulders sagged. "No."

"Then, my dear, experience should tell you that it won't change my plans for tonight. I want you to see what an amazing future you have in movies. You're a star! We can be like those reviewers on television, both saying what we like and what we don't like about each scene. Of course, that'll be from a totally outside objective view. What we like while making the movies, our subjective preferences, will be incredibly obvious. Oh, you'll see in a few minutes." He released his hold, allowing her to settle onto one of the large, overstuffed seats. Although her eyes were downcast, wetness covered her cheeks, and her shoulders shuddered in silence. He chuckled. "Since you didn't eat, and this is like a premiere, would you like me to call the kitchen for popcorn?"

She shook her head. The movement was so slight. Had it not been for the movement of her hair hanging over her face, he wouldn't have seen it.

Tony cleared his throat, reached for her chin, and brushed the renegade strands away. He wasn't going to allow her to hide her thoughts from him. There was too much happening behind those damn green windows. His words came slowly, deliberately, and with painstaking control. "I asked you a question. Do you really want me to repeat it?"

"No, I heard you." Her voice grew stronger, starting at a whisper and becoming bold. "No, I don't want popcorn. I want this over." She started to stand. "I don't want it over!" She looked him in the eye. "I don't want it to start!"

His chest met hers. "But it will." His tone left no room for debate.

Obediently, her knees buckled and she collapsed back into her soft chair.

As Tony reached for the remote, Claire asked, "Why? What's the point in this? I know what's happened. Why do you want me to see it?"

His sinister smile returned, as did the tightness in his slacks. If Claire hadn't been so preoccupied, she'd undoubtedly have noticed. "You seemed surprised that these videos exist. I want you to understand: I'm a man of my word. If I say something exists, it exists. If I say you will do something, you will do it. There are no gray areas. Do you understand?"

"I do." She wiped her eyes with the back of her hand. "I didn't doubt you." Crying interrupted her speech. "I-I *don't* doubt you." More tears. "I don't need to see."

"That's enough," he growled. He was done talking and done listening.

Tony hit a button on the remote, lowered the lights in the room, and opened the video library menu. He leaned over to emphasize his point. "I'm not interested in hearing any more. Don't push me further." She didn't speak; instead, she swallowed, nodded, and tilted her tear-dampened face toward the screen which now contained dates and locations.

He'd given this a lot of thought. They had all night to view. *So why not start at the beginning?* Tony chose *2010, March 20, S.E Suite,* and programmed the time: *8:00 AM*. Before he hit *ENTER*, he glanced in her direction. The look he saw told him that she knew the date—and already knew what she was about to see.

The screen came to life; it was Claire's suite:

She was wearing a white robe and lay curled up on the floor near the hall door. There was a beep and the door opened. Claire jumped, hearing the sound and seeing Tony enter.

"Good morning, Claire." Claire looked at him.

"Good morning, Anthony. I want you to know, I've decided to go home. I'll be leaving here today."

He couldn't contain the chuckle that rose in the back of his throat. Obviously, things didn't proceed as she'd planned.

On the screen, with his eyes dark, he smiled and spoke, "Do you not like your accommodations?" He didn't wait for her to answer. "I don't believe you'll be leaving so soon. We have a legally binding agreement..." He took a bar napkin from his suit pocket. "...dated and signed by both of us."

"Please, Tony. I don't want to see this." Claire covered her eyes with her hands.

He'd warned her to stop this ridiculous display. Roughly grasping her wrists, he pulled them away from her eyes. Through clenched teeth he growled, "I promised a viewing. I said you would watch—and you *will* watch."

He tightly held her wrists to her lap as the video progressed in real time:

Claire was speaking, her voice high-pitched and filled with desperation. "It is not the end of this discussion. This is ludicrous. An agreement doesn't give you the right to rape me! I'm leaving."

Tony's hand contacted Claire's left cheek.

Tony released Claire's wrists and her hand moved to her cheek. He watched to be sure she wasn't trying to cover her eyes again, but she wasn't. Looking back to the screen, he saw himself talking:

"Perhaps in time your memory will improve. It seems to be an issue. Let me remind you again, rule number one is that you do as you are told. If I say a discussion is over, it is over, and this written agreement, which states whatever is pleasing to me, means consensual, not rape. I've decided that it would be better if you didn't leave your suite for a while. Don't worry; we have plenty of time—$215,000 worth of time." Tony looked down. Under his shoes was broken crystal. He continued speaking. "I'll tell the staff that you may have your breakfast after you clean up this crystal."

He left Claire's room.

"Please stop the video!" Claire cried. "Please, I can't watch anymore."

He hit the button and the menu reappeared. "Oh, there're so many videos." His amusement was clear. "We can watch for hours. For example..." The screen read *March 19, 2010.* "...how do you suppose your suite got into that condition? I'm sure we could find out."

"Please!" she pleaded. "Please... you're leaving tomorrow. Wouldn't you rather spend tonight making movies instead of watching?"

When Claire sprang from her chair, Tony was about to follow and reprimand; instead, she fell to the floor and kneeled at his feet. Desperation emanated from every fiber of her being, from her red and puffy eyes to her runny nose. Not since she first arrived had he seen her so broken. Tony smirked. She was a far cry from the confident woman in her suite, just a few nights ago.

He leaned down and teased, purposely pushing her further. "Maybe we should watch some more—find out where you need improvement."

"I'll do anything you say, anything you want me to do differently—just tell me. Just *please* don't make me watch."

He sat back and looked at her. Truly, the dramatics were growing old. "You *will* do whatever I say, even if it is to watch, but," he hesitated to add emphasis, "I don't want to spend my last night here, for over a week, with you in this condition." As he stood, he callously brushed her from his lap, causing her to fall back onto the carpet. "I'll be in your suite in a few minutes."

Claire stood.

Tony continued, "Go up and get ready. Wash your face! You look like hell, and as far as attire... I'm thinking some new lingerie."

When she started to leave the theater, Tony gripped her arm and stalled her steps. His grip tightened as she met his gaze. They'd been through this too many times. "Claire, what do you say?"

Suddenly, he saw the fire from behind the tears as her neck straightened. It took a moment, but finally she was able to articulate the pleasantries he sought. "Thank you, Tony."

Damn her and damn that fire. He loosened his grip. "You may demonstrate your gratitude when I get upstairs."

He watched as she stood motionless. As the silence grew, the fire smoldered to mere embers. It was then that he instructed her movement. "You have been dismissed. You may go to your suite now."

Chapter 5

Promises made—August 2010

(Consequences—Chapter 14)

———◦◦◆◦◦———

For every promise, there is a price to pay.
—Jim Rohn

TONY WASN'T SURE what to expect, or even what he wanted to find, as he walked down the S.E. corridor. He didn't need to check the monitors; Catherine had informed him as soon as he arrived that Claire was waiting for him in her suite. Apparently, Claire had asked Catherine about his arrival, and Catherine had said that she didn't know the particulars.

This was the longest they'd been separated since he brought her to his estate. There'd been occasions when he'd left for a day or two due to business obligations, but this separation had been ten days. Before he left, they'd had another *glitch*, and he didn't leave her in the best condition. Oh, physically she was fine. Her acquired cooperation over the last five months had greatly reduced the need for physical assertiveness, beyond what came in the heat of the moment. No, when Tony left Claire, she was emotionally spent.

Breaking her spirit had been his goal, and in true Anthony

Rawlings fashion, he succeeded. He remembered every minute, both in his theater and in her suite. Tony pushed Claire to a place she didn't want to go. He'd exhibited his power and watched as the fire behind her green eyes dimmed. Then, he purposely dowsed it some more. He remembered the note he'd left on her table:

I believe we have a blockbuster on our hands.
*It's hard to say, until we **thoroughly review the footage. I*
plan to return a week from Wednesday. Eric is available if
you want to visit the Quad Cities. I trust last night's film
*reminded you of my rules. Don't disappoint me.***

He left that with the intention of quenching any renegade sparks. At the time, it had been invigorating.

Then he left and—almost immediately—the elation faded.

Tony didn't doubt his power—it was obvious. He had the ability to make Claire's world heaven or hell; however, for a reason that Tony didn't fully comprehend, that control didn't satisfy him the way it once had. From the beginning of her acquisition, he'd thought of it like a business deal. He made those every day. Companies were bought and sold. They were expanded or the doors were closed. Employees benefited or suffered—it happened.

Tony told himself over and over that Claire's role was nothing more than that of an employee—maybe less. Therefore, when his procurement was complete, when he'd succeeded and broken her spirit, he should've experienced the euphoria that accompanied a hard-fought gain. In the case of this acquisition, taking Claire's mind and spirit had been more difficult than taking her body. It would seem as though his jubilation should've lasted longer than the car ride to the plane. It didn't.

Without warning, uneasiness settled in.

It wasn't that Tony missed Claire while he was in Europe; nevertheless, she continually infiltrated his thoughts. After a day or two, he decided to check the feed from her suite, believing it would satisfy his curiosity and allow him to concentrate on the matters at hand. Since there was a seven-hour time difference between Switzerland and Iowa, the morning that he peered into his iPad, he found Claire peacefully asleep in her bed. Obviously, she wasn't having the same insomnia issues that had plagued him.

The small peek helped. Although he wasn't able to keep Claire out of his thoughts, now those thoughts were images of her sleeping. He'd be negotiating or discussing something with someone and the satin strap of her nightgown, which had been barely visible on his small screen, would come to mind. He'd close his eyes and see her relaxed expression. If he concentrated long enough, Tony was sure that he could smell her scent, a fragrant mixture of perfume, hairspray, and sex. He'd imagine what it was like sleeping with her and removing the satin and lace from her soft skin. Although he enjoyed the way the negligees hugged her curves, they were merely for show. When he was home, she rarely spent the night actually sleeping in them.

Then, as his day progressed, his newfound peace faded. Each time he checked the feed from her suite, even late into his evening, he found the room empty. With time-lapsed speed, he saw the cleaning staff, but Claire was absent. The last image he found of her was before 9:00 AM in Iowa.

As he was about to retire, around midnight in Geneva, Claire's suite was still empty. It didn't make sense. It was almost 5:00 PM in Iowa City, and she should be there—it was her job! Nevertheless, she wasn't. Tony checked the library, the theater, the pool, and the gardens. He couldn't locate her on any monitors.

Then he remembered his note. He'd told Claire that Eric was available to her while he was gone. Assuring himself that she was only out shopping and safely with Eric, Tony tried to go to sleep. Behind his closed eyes, images of her sleeping with her sun-lightened hair fanned over her pillow and that damn satin strap fought for contention with his new worries and concerns regarding her whereabouts. Finally, he gave into his curiosity and called Eric.

"Yes, Mr. Rawlings?"

"I was checking to see where you've taken Ms. Claire in my absence, and to learn if you're nearly back to the estate."

"Sir?"

Uncharacteristically, Tony's voice reflected his concerns. "Ms. Claire. I told her that you'd be available if she wanted to leave the estate. You have accompanied her, haven't you? You know not to let her out by herself."

"Sir, I do know her limitations. However, she's not requested to leave the estate. I haven't taken her anywhere."

"She wasn't with you today, for most of the day, and currently?"

"No, sir," Eric replied. "I can go to the main house and locate her for you, if you'd like?"

Tony decided to go another direction. Dismissing Eric, he disconnected the line. His chest felt tight as he fought to inhale. Ignoring his physical discomfort, he walked down the hall to the small liquor cabinet in the sitting room of his suite. The bottle clinked the crystal as his unsteady hand poured two fingers of bourbon into the tumbler. The smooth amber fluid numbed his throat and calmed his nerves as it disappeared in one swallow. He poured another glass and reached for his phone. With steadier fingers, he retrieved Catherine's personal number and hit CALL.

Catherine informed him that Claire was spending her days hiking.

Hiking? What the hell? To where? To whom?

Catherine only said that Claire took a lunch and returned each day by 6:00 PM.

That night, he tossed and turned until he had visual confirmation of her return. It was nearly 2:00 AM in Geneva, and Tony wasn't sure who deserved to be reprimanded for this breach, Claire or Catherine. The next evening, Tony cut a dinner engagement short, claiming an exorbitant amount of work with a deadline quickly approaching, to sit in his suite and review days of video. Upon further investigation, he found what he wanted. Starting on the Monday after he left, and each morning following, at approximately 9:00 AM, Claire would walk along the garden path and quietly step through the perimeter of trees. Something in his chest clutched each time he watched her disappear into the shaded darkness.

On the fifth day he called Catherine again. It was after 11:00 PM in Switzerland, and he may have had more than a few fingers of bourbon. "Is she back?"

"Isn't your Internet working?"

"Don't be a smart-ass. I'm concerned that you're becoming lax in your judgment."

"May I remind you that you were the one to approve the hikes in the first place? She reminded me of that."

"Walks into the woods—not day-long excursions!"

Catherine's response was more of a sound than a word.

Tony's liquored tongue enunciated perfectly, and his words dripped with sarcasm. "I watched the exchange between the two of you on the day I left. Weren't you just the sweetest?"

"I can be," Catherine responded. "Would you have rather I did nothing and she went mad?"

This time Tony made the noise. "It wasn't that bad," he scoffed.

"It was. She was on the edge of a very dark place. I know the signs. I just helped her see that she could survive."

"I didn't think that was your goal."

Catherine allowed the line to go silent. Finally she replied, "I've grown used to her."

"Used to her? Like a pet?" He knew better than to bring up the motherly comment again.

Catherine murmured under her breath. Apparently, she didn't see his obvious restraint. He changed his tone. "What if she decides to leave the property?"

"She's returned every day, with minutes to spare."

"Hmm." He assessed. "At least she's a well-trained pet, but why? Why is she doing this, and where is she going?"

"I can only assume to gain some sense of personal freedom. She knows that her suite is monitored, and she feels she can have some time to herself beyond the perimeter of the grounds."

Tony thought about Catherine's response. It made sense, but he didn't like it. He didn't want her to have that freedom. He wanted all of her. Perhaps it was the liquor, but his tone softened. "Do you think it's helped her?"

"I do. She seems different, resigned to her fate, yet I don't know— stronger."

"And do you know where she goes? My property goes on for miles."

"I don't know. The laundry staff has informed me of bathing suits. Perhaps she's sunbathing?"

"She can do that at the pool," Tony answered, as images of Claire, wearing one of her many bathing suits, lying near the pool, paraded through his consciousness.

"Do you want me to tell her that she's no longer allowed to

go on her hikes?"

He contemplated. "You said she's home every night by 6:00 PM. Why not 5:00 PM?"

"I told her 6:00 PM. You aren't here. She dines alone."

He nodded. "All right, no. Don't stop her as long as she follows your rules. Catherine?"

"Yes?"

"On the day of my arrival, do not tell her when I'll be in. Don't even remind her of my day of arrival. I want to see if she'll be ready. I want to know that she'll be following my rules. She knows that if I'm to be home, she's to be available. Let's see what she'll do with this new personal freedom and how far she'll take it."

"All right, Anton. If that's what you want."

"I do."

He hit DISCONNECT.

As Tony's hand touched the lever of Claire's door, he took a deep breath. Perhaps, just perhaps, what Anthony Rawlings feared was that ten days ago he *had* succeeded. There was something about Claire's resilience, something about her strength in the face of his tyranny, that intrigued him. It was a game and he enjoyed the invigorating play.

Ten days ago, Claire seemed defeated even before he showed her the videos. *If he had totally broken her spirit, would the game be done? Then what would he do? If she were emotionally as accommodating as she was physically, would the challenge be over?*

Tony couldn't remember another time in his life when he wanted so desperately to have failed. Opening the door, he panned the suite and found Claire seated on the sofa with a book. Exhaling, he stepped forward, knowing that he'd have to face the consequences of his actions. Their eyes met and his back straightened. Tony knew. He could see it in those damn green eyes—her fire was back!

"Good afternoon, Claire."

Her movements were deliberate and slow. She placed her bookmark in her book, laid the book on the end table, and stood. "Good afternoon, Anthony. It's nice to have you home. How was your trip?"

He stepped forward, wanting—no needing—to gauge her reaction. The scent of her perfume intensified with each step. When he was mere inches away, he stopped. This proximity required her to look up to maintain eye contact. Without direction, her chin rose defiantly, her lips held the perfect smile, and her eyes screamed with the intensity he sought. As much as he wanted to pull her into his arms, he heard himself bait her. It was his game and he couldn't stop. "My trip was long. I'm pleased with your greeting. Does this mean your temper tantrum from before my trip has reached its conclusion?"

"Yes, I believe it has. I apologize for my behavior. It was childish and unnecessary."

He had failed to break her—or so it seemed; nevertheless, Tony needed to push and learn if Claire was truly as fragile and on the edge as Catherine said, or if her spirit was renewed. He grinned. "As I recall, a great deal of your behavior was far from childish..." he paused—no reaction, "...but my memory could be failing me. It has been a long trip. I know how we could find out..." another pause—no reaction, "...or review?"

She didn't take his bait. Instead, she responded, "You're right. It was very adult. I'd be glad to do whatever it is you tell me to do again. I believe I have a debt to repay. My goal is to make that happen sooner rather than later. Fulfilling my contract is the means to that end."

He couldn't fight the urge any longer. He had failed—and he'd never been so relieved. Swiftly, he pulled her against him and watched the fire rage. Oh, she smiled, said all the right things, but her damn eyes were fighting. It was better than he'd dared to hope. Bending down, his lips captured hers. *Did he sense hesitation?* If so, it was briefly lived. Suddenly, she was pressing back with equal force. He lifted her petite frame and held tight to her firm, round behind as her arms encircled his neck.

All of the trepidation he'd felt walking the gauntlet from his office to her suite morphed into unbridled desire. He didn't want to make her watch movies; he wanted to make them. *Would he watch them?* Probably, but that wasn't what he was thinking as he backed her against the beige wall and her legs encircled his torso. He was silently cursing her choice of attire. Tony would give his entire fortune for her to be wearing a skirt.

It didn't take long and the damn white slacks and slippery blouse were history, lost somewhere on the floor of her suite. His suit followed, as Claire met him move for move. She was careful not to initiate, but whatever he suggested, whether it was verbal or otherwise, she met him head-on. As the afternoon progressed, he silently questioned if the Claire he'd hope to find was back, or if this was someone different, someone stronger? He wasn't sure, and he didn't waste too much time wondering.

About 6:30 PM, he used his cell phone to call the kitchen and have dinner brought to her suite. The flight had been long and their reunion exhausting. It was about 9:30 PM when he finally succumbed to sleep. In the moment before sweet nothingness prevailed and Tony slept better than he had in over a week, the satin strap he'd seen in the video feed crossed his mind. Taking one last glance toward Claire, he saw her bare shoulders and grinned. Tonight she wouldn't be wearing a nightgown to sleep.

TONY'S SHOES ECHOED against the marble floor of the long corridor as he made his way toward the front staircase. Inklings of crimson seeped into his vision as each step pounded more determined than the last. All day long, he'd thought about his reunion with Claire and her change in demeanor. As the day progressed he'd convinced himself not only of her acceptance of her situation, but the obvious pleasure she derived from it. Then, as if to prove him wrong, he went to her suite to retrieve her for dinner, and she was gone. Catherine had assured him that Claire knew dinner was at 7:00 PM. *Where the hell was she?*

Reaching the bottom of the stairs, he was about to call out to Catherine, when Tony stopped. In the sitting room, waiting calmly, dressed appropriately for dinner, was Claire. He stood for a moment and watched as he remained hidden from her view. She had her shapely legs crossed at her ankles, just above her high heels and her hands rested serenely on her lap. The dress she'd chosen to wear was blue and sleeveless, accentuating her tanned, firm arms. She didn't appear anxious, yet she wasn't overtly relaxed—she just *was*. As he stared, the red faded from his view. Tony reasoned that Claire hadn't disobeyed; it was only different. She'd never before taken the initiative to come down to dinner on her own, but there she was. Taking a deep breath, he straightened his suit jacket and stepped into the sitting room. Her eyes immediately went to his. "Good evening, Claire."

She stood and walked toward him. "Good evening, Anthony."

Offering his arm, she rested her small hand in the crook of his elbow, and they walked to the dining room. As they entered, he said, "I went to your suite expecting to find you there."

Her painted eyes widened. "I apologize. I was told dinner would be in the dining room at 7:00 PM; *I didn't want to be late.*"

As he pulled out her chair and she sat, Tony studied the ringlets of hair that teasingly grazed her neck. He reminded himself that the blonde hair emerging from her brown was an outward sign of the new woman he was creating. Her obvious emphasis of obedience was because it was what he demanded—the old Claire wouldn't have done that, perhaps not even recently. This Claire knew her place, and after their glitch a week ago, she was being extra careful.

He sat and studied his creation. He wanted to believe her; yet the red loomed nearby. He found his businessman's tone. "Your punctuality is duly noted. It seems my absence has helped you remember who's in charge and what guidelines you are to follow."

"Yes, your absence was advantageous on many counts."

He stared. *What the hell?* Unable to form a rebuttal that would facilitate their dinner conversation, he waited.

Finally, she spoke again, "I believe it helped me recognize I owe you much, not just the money to repay my debt, but the confidence you've shown in me... the confidence to trust me with your intimate beliefs." She paused. "I will not betray that confidence."

While Cindy and Carlos entered the dining room and filled the table with food and drinks, Tony continued to stare. He looked for any sign of manipulation. *Truly, what did she expect to gain?* Once they were again alone, Tony said, "Claire, if you're sincere, you never cease to amaze me. If, however, you're playing me, you will regret it."

"Tony, what would I gain by playing you? I'm aware my present, future, and release are solely in your hands. I'm sorry for my behavior before you left."

He broke their gaze as he contemplated her words. Her eyes had been in agreement: he saw spirit, but not fight. Tony didn't accept her declaration, but he didn't rebuke it either. He changed the subject and they ate.

After dinner he escorted her out to the gardens for a stroll. As they approached the area in the path where he'd watch her disappear, he stopped. The underbrush was down trodden. He gazed into the trees. With the setting sun, the woods appeared dark and unknown, yet he knew she'd been there every day. *Why?*

She looked from the point in the border of the trees and then up to him. When she didn't volunteer, Tony asked, "Tell me about your walks. How far do you go?"

"I'm not sure... in miles. At first, I just walked."

"At first?"

"At first, I was trying to get a feel of your land and would go in different directions. I found the most beautiful clearings, right in the middle of the trees. There were flowers, wild flowers, and..." He listened to her words, but there was something else, a sense of discovery or wonder that he'd never heard or seen before—in anyone. They were just damn trees and bugs and things that existed wherever man had yet to build something truly spectacular; however, as she described the clearings, the insects, and animals, her eyes—no, her whole damn face—lit up like she was describing the most beautiful monuments in the world. "...that's when I found the lake. Oh, Tony, it's beautiful. It isn't big, but it isn't small. There're fish and a beach. I've been taking books and reading and enjoying the sun."

"A lake?" he questioned. "I remember seeing one, years ago, when I did flyovers of the land to help me decide where to have the house built."

Her look of wonder morphed into one of blatant concern. "I-Is it still on your land?"

He took her hand in his. "Yes," he reassured. "That's still on my land. You haven't broken my rules."

Claire's obvious relief was the final shove to push the red away. Maybe it was as Catherine said, *he was used to her, or maybe he had missed her? Had she missed him? He didn't want to ask. Even if he did ask, could he believe her answer? If she were truthful and the answer wasn't what he wanted—it was better not to ask.*

Tony reached into his breast pocket and brought out a black velvet box. "I found these for you in Italy. I thought they made a nice complement to your necklace."

Claire hesitantly accepted the small box. Before she opened it, she peered up at him through her lashes. It struck him again how different she was from the other women he'd dated. They would've never hesitated; they wanted gifts, the more the better. Then again, he and Claire weren't dating—were they?

She opened the box and revealed the pearl earrings he'd found at a small jewelry store in Florence. He'd seen them in the window and immediately thought of Claire's necklace. They weren't exactly the same; however, the pearls were very similar and they were offset on white gold circles. He explained, "Your necklace is a cross, which is an X on its side. Now your earrings are O's—X's and O's." He smiled.

"Thank you, Tony," she said as she closed the lid. "It was very kind of you to think of me during your busy trip."

He placed her hand back into the crook of his arm, and they continued to walk about the garden. The sun was setting and he was home.

Chapter 6

A day with friends—September 2010

(Consequences—Chapter 15)

———————◆———————

A single moment of misunderstanding can be
so poisonous that it can make us forget the
many loveable moments spent together.
—Melchor Lim

"I WON THAT one," Tony said, as he handed Tim the pool cue. "You'd better keep the winning streak going against Tom in this next game, or I may have to look for a new vice president."

Tom heard Tony's jovial tone and joined the fun. "It's all right, Tim: Tony'll give you a good reference," he laughed, "as long as the company isn't looking for a pool shark."

Tim smiled. "Oh, I'm not worried. You haven't seen my mad skills. I'm pretty sure I'll be gainfully employed come tomorrow."

Brent nudged Tony and whispered, "I like his confidence."

"Yeah, the kid's got something. I'm glad Courtney let you invite him."

Brent shrugged.

Eli called from the poker table on the other side of the room. "Hey, who's ready to lose some money? Chance and I have the chips ready."

Brent cocked his eyebrow toward Tony. "I think it's time to show them who's the real master of the cards."

"Maybe we should go easy on them?" Tony suggested.

"Nah," they both said in unison.

When they neared the poker table, Tony hesitated. "Deal a few hands without me. I'm gonna go upstairs for a minute."

"There's more beer behind the bar," Brent offered.

Tony looked down at his nearly full bottle. "I'm good. It's your wife's great cooking—I'm gonna go grab some of that cheese dip."

Brent eyed him suspiciously. "Sure, you know the way, but hurry back after you check on your gal. We'll be waiting."

Tony stared at his friend for a moment. *His gal? Not even close. "Companion." That was the description he'd decided upon.* "Whatever." He shrugged. "I like cheese dip."

With that, he set his beer on the nearest table and walked up the stairs. As he rounded the hallway toward the kitchen, the sound of voices stilled his progress. From his vantage, he could only hear the women. All at once, MaryAnn's voice prevailed as she went on at some length about one of Eli's clients—some movie star who apparently had a body *to die for.* Tony waited and listened as other voices added their opinions. With each passing comment that wasn't Claire's, Tony thought more and more about her restraint. He wasn't sure that the woman he acquired in Atlanta would have remained quiet for so long. The longer her voice remained absent, the more his newfound pride gave way to a growing wave of panic. *What if she wasn't speaking because she wasn't there? What if she'd found a way to leave—a way of escape? Would she do that?*

Determinedly, he turned the corner, hoping for visual confirmation of her presence. Though she was sitting facing out to the backyard, he immediately saw her profile. Nestled in the corner of the wicker loveseat, she was tracing the rim of her wine glass with her finger and listening as everyone discussed the sexy movie star. As he watched, she kept her eyes focused on the women and attentively followed the conversation. For a split second he thought of the woman he met at the Red Wing. The two Claires seemed worlds apart. It wasn't just appearance, although this Claire was toner, tanner, and blonder—all qualities he appreciated. The streaks of yellow that highlighted her hair were probably his favorite change; that's why he'd offered to take her to Chicago. The sun would soon lose its intensity, and that blonde would need help. This Claire was also more refined and genteel: she didn't burst into conversations or talk excessively. Well, she did talk more when they were alone, but the woman on the sunporch knew her role. Just as he was about to step further into the kitchen, he heard her name.

"So, Claire, what's your opinion? He's pretty hot, isn't he?" There was something about Bonnie's voice that grated on Tony's nerves. He wished that Eli and MaryAnn could have made the trip without these tagalongs.

Tony saw Claire's smile; it wasn't as genuine as the one she flashed him earlier in the car, but that didn't detract from its beauty. She had no idea he was watching or listening as she answered, "Oh, yes, he's hot! But I haven't seen the movie." Looking toward MaryAnn, she apologized: "I'm sorry. I'm just not much of a moviegoer."

Tony knew that was true now, but when he'd watched her in Atlanta, she used to go to the movies frequently with her friends. He remembered taking her to a movie—their private viewing—about a month ago. He quickly pushed the memory away. It wasn't as pleasant as it had once been.

"Is Tony?" Bonnie pried. "Is he a moviegoer? What do you two like to do?"

Before Claire could answer, Sue chimed in. "Well, let me tell you—

I saw the movie last week. It isn't Tim's kind of movie, so I went with a friend..."

Tony quit listening as an arm brushed his waist. Turning, he saw Courtney as she leaned toward him and whispered, "So, where did you find her?"

"What?"

Courtney stood back and looked him straight in the eye. "She's not your type," her serious expression turned joyous, "and that's a good thing. I like her a lot."

"You do? And what do you mean—*my type*? I didn't know I had a *type*."

"Well, you do, and most of them wouldn't be caught dead sitting on my sunporch chatting. Claire's sweet. I'll admit, when Brent told me that you took her to New York for business, I was skeptical." She put her hand on his. "I mean, you know we care about you. It's just that, well, some of the women you've dated—"

Tony interrupted, "So, you're now telling me that you don't approve of my choices?" Though his words could be considered accusatory, his tone was soft and playful.

"Well, it probably isn't my place, but someone has to keep you in line." Her smile twinkled in her blue eyes. "Claire's young, but I think she might be a keeper. I've never seen you like this before."

"Like what?"

"Look at you. You're up here checking on her. What's the matter, are you afraid she's gonna learn some of your dark secrets and bolt?" Courtney leaned closer. "Don't worry, she's safe with us."

"I wasn't checking on her. I-I was getting something to eat." As soon as the words rolled off his tongue, he realized the food had all been put away.

"Oh, my mistake." Her grin clearly displayed her disbelief of his cover story. "I guess it was your swooning and eavesdropping that had me confused."

Courtney didn't know how wrong she was, or perhaps *why* she was wrong. Tony *was* checking on her—her *presence* and her *behavior*. After all, it was the first time he'd allowed her this much freedom with anyone other than his house staff, and it was more than a bit disconcerting. Even when they were out at fundraisers, or she was shopping, she was never with anyone long enough to discuss her situation. He sure as hell didn't want her discussing it now. He shifted his glance back to Courtney who'd quickly moved to the refrigerator. As she opened the large door, she asked, "Now, what was it that you wanted to eat?"

He knew he'd been caught; there was no reason to go on with the charade. Laughingly, he replied, "Don't go to any bother. I think I'm fine."

Claire must have heard the sound of their voices; when he turned back toward the porch she was looking right at him. Her lips smiled; however, her eyes questioned—seeking his approval. Without thinking, he smiled. Claire's shoulders relaxed as she placed her glass on the table, still looking in his direction, and started to stand. Shaking his head, he waved her off. Obediently, she picked up her glass and sat back against the cushion. He'd heard enough of the conversation to know she was performing well, and he didn't want to interrupt the ladies' discussion.

When he looked back at Courtney, she was staring at him.

Before she could speak, he said, "Um, I'm going back downstairs."

"Yes, you do that. I hope you liked your snack."

If it were almost anyone else, Tony would have been upset—but not with Courtney. He truly did value her and Brent's friendship. When he told Claire they were some of his *closest friends,* he'd been sincere. There was something about Courtney that lit up a room. While others seemed nervous or apprehensive in Tony's presence, she never did. He admired her for that.

Walking toward the lower level, he thought about Courtney's assessment of Claire. It both puzzled and pleased him. He'd been apprehensive about bringing Claire to this barbeque—not that he doubted her ability to perform; over the past almost six months she'd improved exponentially. It was more a concern that Courtney would see through the facade. The fact that she didn't *and* she approved of Claire was food for thought.

He entered the lower level just in time to watch Tim lift his pool cue and point. "Eight ball, corner pocket."

Seconds later, the black ball bounced from one bumper to the next, successfully avoiding the scattered striped balls, and fell effortlessly into the corner hole. Shaking his head, Tom said, "I believe I've just been schooled by the schoolboy."

Feeling easier about Claire's behavior, Tony slapped Tim on the back. "Good job, I believe you can be assured your position is safe. Just don't start thinking you can challenge me to a game of eight ball to move higher in Rawlings. I'm not planning on handing over the reins any day soon."

The evening sky began to darken as everyone sat around Brent's fire pit. As much as Tony enjoyed the camaraderie of the day, he couldn't stop thinking about getting Claire home and telling her what an amazing job she'd done. Yes, *telling* wasn't the only thing on his mind. He fully intended on *showing* her. It wasn't a plan of appreciation. She'd done what she needed to do. It was a plan of positive reinforcement. In a few short hours, she'd seemed to charm not only Courtney, but all of his friends.

Courtney had been right when she said that most of the women he dated weren't the type to sit contentedly around a fire pit and listen to stories. They were women who liked to be wined and dined and who enjoyed all that his money could buy. The people present had no way of knowing that this outing meant more to Claire than a diamond bracelet. They had no way of knowing that it was her first experience in a long time that involved this many people. Squeezing Claire's shoulder, he couldn't help but smile when she looked his way. The day had been truly more than he imagined or expected. He whispered, "We should be going."

Although Claire showed a twinge of disappointment, a microsecond later it turned into a complying nod and smile. She knew better than to argue, especially in a non-private setting. The other voices from around the fire were the ones who chimed in with their disappointment. They all wanted Tony and Claire to stay longer.

"It has been wonderful to get to know all of you," Claire said seconds before Courtney swallowed her in a hug.

"Thank you for coming, and make sure Tony brings you around more often," Courtney said as she peered over Claire's shoulder and winked at Tony. When the two women ended their embrace, Courtney continued speaking to Tony, "And don't scare her off. I like her."

While he shrugged innocently, he looked up in time to see Sue hand Claire a piece of paper. As Claire opened it, Sue said, "Call me; we can do lunch."

The next few minutes were a blur. Tony's need for appearances kicked in, and his actions and words were on autopilot. As he remained polite and said his goodbyes, his mind swirled with thoughts about the note. *What did it say? What had Claire and Sue talked about?* He walked Claire to the car and opened her door. *Did he assist her in getting in?* Tony couldn't remember. The moment he maneuvered the Lexus off Brent's property, his ingrained concern with appearances evaporated—it was just Claire and him. They were no longer among others. Though the sun had set, the fall evening filled with a hue of red as they drove silently along the country roads. He made no attempt to rein in the threatening rage. *How had the perfect day changed so drastically?*

Tony didn't know how far or how long he'd driven before he abruptly pulled the car onto the shoulder. Dirt and rocks pelted the underside of the convertible as he slammed his foot on the brake and threw the gearshift into *PARK*. There were too many things running through his mind, too many questions, and too many possibilities. He imagined the conversation between Claire and the wife of his vice president.

"I'm not his companion; he kidnapped me. Can you please help me? He isn't like you think!"

The prospects were limitless. Instead of speaking, Tony held out his hand—he couldn't even look at her, not after what she'd done.

"Tony..." she began, as she handed him the piece of paper.

He didn't give Claire the chance to continue. With the hand that held Sue's note, he seized her mouth and squeezed her cheeks. If he covered her nose... no, that wasn't what he wanted. At the moment he didn't know what he wanted. He just knew the perfect day had gone to hell in a matter of seconds.

"Not now," he managed through gritted teeth. "We'll discuss this when we get home." Prying his hand from her face, he resumed his grip on the steering wheel. They rode in silence until they reached the front door of the estate.

Before they arrived at the Simmons' house, Tony had made Claire a deal. *Was it a deal—or perhaps a threat?* Either way, he'd promised her a day at the spa in Chicago—*if* she behaved. When he stopped the car, he didn't bother to open her door. *This wasn't a damn date.* He kept his eyes fixed straight ahead and said, "Go up to your suite. I'll be up soon; in the meantime, I have things to do, like cancel a spa appointment."

Though he didn't turn, he knew she wanted to speak, possibly explain. It took her a few seconds, but soon, Claire opened her door and walked toward the house—out of the corner of his eye, he saw her head high and shoulders back. Her arrogance in the face of his power only fueled his thoughts. *If she were brazen enough to respond like that when she knew she was about to be punished, what would she risk to get free?*

———◆———

HE'D WATCHED HER for over an hour on the monitors. Catherine had even come into his office and tried to learn the reason for his change in demeanor. He couldn't or didn't want to explain. He couldn't tell Catherine that she'd been right all along, that Claire had just been holding back, waiting for the opportunity to get free and take him down in the process. Tony didn't want to admit that to himself, much less someone else. After all, he'd taken her to his friends—*to his best friends*—and now look what she'd done!

His decision was made. Behaviors had consequences and she needed to be punished. *How?* He debated, until he realized that punishment wasn't something to be thought out; it was something to be delivered swiftly when necessary. It was a means by which to curb unacceptable behavior. What she had done or said while with Sue was undoubtedly unacceptable. Claire knew the rules: no divulging of private information. If Sue wanted to have lunch—there would obviously be sharing of private information, if there hadn't been already.

By the time Tony stepped through the door of her suite, he'd decided to allow Claire to choose her penalty: a time-out or corporal punishment. By making her part of the decision process, she was forced to accept her responsibility for her actions, ultimately admitting to her insubordination and agreeing to the consequences.

Tony knew from the monitors that Claire was out on the balcony. The sound of the door must have gotten her attention. He didn't speak, but he stopped and stared in her direction. It was an unspoken command, and she heard it loud and clear. With her back straight and her eyes locked on him, she boldly walked within inches. He lifted her chin, leaned forward, and bathed her cheeks in his warm breath. Tony didn't want there to be any misunderstanding: she had failed to maintain her side of this agreement, and there would be a price to pay. "What did we discuss just before we arrived at the barbeque?"

Her eyes flashed fire, but her words sounded respectful. "I told you I wouldn't let you down and I didn't."

"Actions have consequences; I've told you that. Why is that difficult for you to understand?"

"Tony, it isn't. If—" He didn't want excuses. The control he'd tried to gather during the drive and in his office evaporated. His open palm struck her cheek. It wasn't powerful enough to knock her down, yet it accomplished his goal—she stopped speaking.

"Actions have consequences," he repeated. As the evidence of his persuasion began to rise on her cheek, her moist eyes stayed fixed on his, and he continued, "I've been thinking quite a bit about an appropriate punishment."

"Tony, if you would please let me speak. I know your decision is set, but allow me to talk."

Her strength was commendable. More out of awe, he nodded and said, "Fine, make it quick." Her words wouldn't matter; his decision was set.

"I was nervous about going to this barbeque today, but I had a wonderful time. Courtney was the perfect hostess and very charming. Everyone was nice to me. I really didn't know what to expect." Her words were barely spaced. "Well, everyone except Bonnie. By the way, I overheard Bonnie and MaryAnn talking and everyone there had your back. That includes me. Sue—well, Sue's lonely. She told me that Tim works long hours, which she mentioned he enjoys, but she's lonely. At some point, she asked me for my number. I don't have one—as you know—but I thought that sounded dumb: everyone has a cell phone. So I just said I didn't have it with me and I didn't know my number. I never call myself. So, I'm guessing that's why she gave me her number. I really didn't know she was going to do it. If I had, would I've had her do it right in front of you?"

He didn't want to hear this—it wasn't the way he had imagined.

Claire went on. "When Courtney introduced me to Tim and Sue, I told Tim I'd heard good things about him—from you. I can only guess that made Sue and I instant friends. Women love to hear good things about their husbands. I would've told you if I'd gotten the number without your knowing. I have no way of calling, and if I just didn't call, it would appear rude. I know how you feel about appearances." Her tone softened. She'd stated her case; this was more of a plea. "I really did well today; this was just a misunderstanding, and your friends were very nice."

Tony looked down into her eyes and tried to retrieve the red her explanation had muted. He wanted to punish her; she deserved it, *didn't she?* He went on with his plan. "I've decided you may choose. Perhaps you would like to know your choices?"

Defeat filled her green eyes. It was the expression she'd had during their dinner, before he showed her the movies. The window into her thoughts disappeared. For the first time since he entered the room, she looked away as helplessness filled her voice. "Tony, your decision is made; I don't care."

"The first option is a two-week time-out in your suite."

Suddenly, the fire was back. She glared, stood, and met him face-to-face. God, her strength captivated him. The defeat was gone. If there was a punishment coming, she wanted to choose. "Then

I choose number two."

He didn't respond. The silence grew. He wanted her. He wanted to tell her he was sorry—he overreacted—but that wasn't him. He couldn't.

"Very well, undress."

She didn't hesitate; she obeyed his command and started by unbuttoning her blouse, one button at a time. Then she shimmied out of her slacks; she didn't argue or complain and maintained eye contact the entire time. Tony's arousal was becoming difficult to conceal. As her body trembled slightly before him, he searched for the red. Like his fury, it was gone. Tony's angry demeanor dissolved.

"Come here," he commanded.

She did. He held her shoulders and looked into her green eyes. "Damn you, Claire." He pulled her close. "I make snap decisions based on the visible evidence. Appearances are important. I assumed you had something planned with Sue—something I hadn't approved. I was wrong. Your speech," he lifted her chin, gently this time, as his tone softened, "was very brave." He watched her expression. "It helped me see that I'd jumped to the wrong conclusion." He put his head down on her hair and the odor of burning wood reminded him of Brent's fire pit. He encircled her body with his arms. She was still trembling and he wanted to warm her.

The memories of the day resurfaced—her smile, the things Courtney and Brent had said, even the fact that Sue wanted to have lunch with her. He was painfully aroused by those thoughts, as well as the soft, naked body in his arms.

Tony's voice continued to mellow. "Up until the moment Sue handed you that note, I was extremely proud of you. You were amazing. Courtney told me that about ten times." He felt the tension leave her body as she became liquid against his chest. Claire lifted her eyes and smiled. He went on. "There's something I'd like us to do."

"Whatever it is—yes."

He'd been wrong, yet instead of being upset, Claire was relieved. He wanted her more than he'd ever wanted her. He no longer tried to subdue his grin as he said, "Your hair smells like smoke. I'd like us to shower."

Returning his grin, Claire took his hand and led him to her bathroom. Once there, she reached for the buttons of his shirt, but before she undid them, her questioning eyes found his. It was a simple unspoken request, and he longed to grant it and more. As she removed his clothes, he undid her braid. Under the warm spray of the shower, he wet her hair, added shampoo, and gently massaged. "Your hair is beautiful, but it needs trimming, and the weather is getting colder, so maybe some highlights. I believe you'll enjoy the spa. It has a great reputation."

Her expression of innocence and surprise about did him in as she turned and asked, "You didn't cancel my appointment?"

"No, I guess I hoped something would change my mind." *Was that true? Had he hoped for that?* Or had he realized that the spa wouldn't be open until the next day? Either way, as he lathered her hair with conditioner and the floral scent replaced the odor of smoke, he was glad he hadn't had the opportunity.

Soon his slippery hands found their way to the curves of her breasts. Despite the warm water, her nipples were taut and hard. Each caress found his hands lower and lower. Turning her around, he lifted her body and held her against the shower wall. She was so light and fit just right. When her legs wrapped around his torso he worked to create the same frenzy in her that he felt burning within. His tongue and teeth taunted her nipples while his fingers increased their pace. By the way her nails gripped his shoulders, he knew she was close to finding the ecstasy that he too wanted to experience.

Adjusting her slightly, he found the place he wanted to be. Her wordless moans filled the shower and pushed him deeper and deeper. All of the day's energies erupted as their bodies quaked in the aftermath of their union. When she laid her head on his shoulder and he heard her ragged breathing, Tony wanted nothing more than to hear those moans of pleasure again.

Through the night, he got what he wanted, and he made sure that Claire did too.

Tony woke before his alarm. Hearing Claire's soft and delicate breathing, he saw her covered with only a sheet and curled into a ball on the far side of the bed. With the pale light of the lingering moon, he noticed her hair fanned around her head, damp and wavy. The sheet did little to hide her petite, soft, and supple body. He carefully lifted the blankets and covered her. As he watched, the warmth of the blankets allowed her to unconsciously relax and settle into a deeper slumber. He wanted her again. He knew he could wake her, and she would accommodate his demands. Laying his head back on the pillow, he remembered the sex they experienced and wondered *when did this happen?* He no longer wanted to dominate but to satisfy.

He hadn't realized the true depth of his feelings until he heard himself apologize. Anthony Rawlings could count on one hand the people to whom he'd apologized. Now this woman—a piece of his plan—was on that shortlist.

Instead of relishing his new realization, he berated himself. Catherine was right: he should have stayed indifferent, dominant, and in charge. *But, wasn't he still in charge?* He was. Even Catherine had said she was used to Claire—so was he.

Maybe he did apologize, and admittedly that was going a bit too far. Words from his past echoed in his memory. "Only the weak apologize." Tony vowed to not allow that to happen again. Glancing again at the woman only a few feet away, he considered waking her. If he did, he could demonstrate the indifferent, domineering qualities that would verify he wasn't weak. He could prove that he was in control.

Seeing her peaceful expression and thinking of her giving and surrendering herself over and over, Tony quietly got out of bed, put on his jeans, and left her suite. Stepping into the corridor, he decided to work out.

Author's Note

This POV was originally written at the request of my amazing readers and appeared in the Goodreads Group: The Consequences Series Group Reads, Therapy, and Hugs. That version has been tweaked and edited for BHE- Consequences. The "Accident" scene in *Consequences* was tragic, difficult to read, difficult to write, and often resulted in my being asked, *"What was Tony thinking?"* I decided to share. This POV was in no way intended to condone abuse or physical violence, but was meant as insight into the troubled mind of a man who experienced pain and betrayal for the first time in his life.

Thank you for joining me on this dark and insightful journey.

~Aleatha

Chapter 7

The Accident—September 2010

(Consequences—Chapter 19)

———◆———

There is no such thing as accident; it is fate misnamed.
—Napoleon Bonaparte

THE WHOLE DAMN deal hung by a thread. How many hours and millions of dollars had been wasted researching and reviewing this investment and securities firm to have it fall apart over some stupid disagreement about benefit buyouts? Sitting at the head of the long conference table, Tony listened to the debate until he couldn't take it any longer. "Ladies and gentlemen," he spoke above the fray, "you have my offer. Your company won't stand as it is another six months. You can either take the deal or file Chapter 11. With my offer your employees will receive appropriate compensation in exchange for their loss of benefits."

"Mr. Rawlings, with all due respect, you're offering pennies on the dollar."

Standing, Tony adjusted his jacket and ignored the vibration of his private cell phone as he replied, "Yes, Mr. Collins, I am. I've also spent over a year learning the ins and outs of your company. You have no other prospects. I suggest you take the offer. The federal bankruptcy courts won't be as generous."

While the murmuring at the conference table intensified, Tony placed the documents and his laptop into his leather briefcase and nodded to his team. Addressing the assembly, he announced, "I expect an answer by tomorrow at noon, or I'll assume that you're taking your chances with the courts. Good day, ladies and gentlemen."

The room fell into a stunned hush as Anthony Rawlings and his protégés gathered their belongings and walked away from the bargaining table. Once they stepped beyond the glass doors and neared the elevator, Tony heard Tom exhale. The team that accompanied him consisted of Tom Miller, his associate, Sharon Michaels, and David Field, one of Tony's negotiators. Only their private assembly entered the small elevator. When the doors shut, Tom leaned toward Tony and spoke in a hushed tone. "I know you know how much it'll cost if this falls through. We're talking about—"

Remaining professional, Tony's eyes met Tom's, interrupting his words. Tony hissed. "I am well aware. We can discuss this further in the office." The conversation was officially stalled. Tony didn't care that it was still early in the afternoon and that their meeting was scheduled to last until much later. He could only present the same information in so many different ways. He had neither the patience nor the inclination to entertain the assholes in that conference room upstairs another minute. They wanted what he wasn't willing to give. He knew that their company needed him more than he needed it. At this point, he needed a few minutes to decompress. If he didn't, he'd be willing to take the whole damn thing as a tax write-off.

The silence continued as they entered the waiting car. They weren't scheduled to return to Iowa until the morning, and they all knew that they'd spend the rest of the day and possibly the night dissecting every last document in their arsenal. Despite Tony's comments, too much had been invested; somewhere there was a definitive piece of information that would insure this deal's success. By all estimations, they had a long night ahead of them.

Just as Tony's nerves began to calm, he again felt his pocket vibrate and reached for his iPhone. Touching the screen, he saw: *TWO TEXT MESSAGES*

Further investigation told him that they both were from his press secretary, Shelly. He read the first:

MR. RAWLINGS PLEASE READ THE ATTACHED PRESS RELEASE THAT JUST CAME ACROSS MY FEED. IT WILL NOT APPEAR FOR A FEW DAYS. IT HAS BEEN PURCHASED BY ROLLING STONE AND PEOPLE. I DON'T THINK I CAN STOP IT.

The car moved in jerky bursts. Tony hated New York City traffic. That was one of the reasons he chose to live in Iowa. Of course, there was traffic there too, but it wasn't this stand-still shit. Instead of reading the attachment, he read the second text, also from his press secretary:

MR. RAWLINGS I'VE CONFIRMED THE SALE OF THE RELEASE TO BOTH MAGAZINES. IF I ATTEMPT TO STOP PUBLICATION IT MAY BACKFIRE. PLEASE ADVISE IMMEDIATELY.

"They're bluffing." Tom's voice broke the silence within the car.

"I don't bluff," Tony replied. "I'd rather lose the preliminary costs than deal with those assholes. I won't be at their mercy. We'll find something that'll make them beg for my offer, and we'll find it tonight."

Tom didn't respond, nor did anyone else. Tony didn't expect responses. After all, he wasn't asking. There was a mission and it would be carried out. When the car stopped in front of the tall office building, Tony and his associates silently entered the building. It was another quiet elevator ride as they made their way to the sixty-second floor and the New York satellite offices of *Rawlings Industries.*

The pretty brunette receptionist immediately stopped her work as Tony and his entourage entered the lobby to the executive offices.

Before she could speak, Tony said, "Kelli, we're planning a long night. Call for food. We'll need sandwiches and coffee delivered."

"I'll get right on that, Mr. Rawlings." Kelli handed him a small stack of papers. "Sir, Shelly has called multiple times. She's very anxious for you to read a press release. I took the liberty of printing it for you."

Taking the printed pages, Tony thanked her and walked into his private office; only Tom followed. He started to sit behind his desk when the title on the page caught his attention. Suddenly, his body ceased to move and the air left his lungs.

"Questions Answered—the Mystery Woman in Anthony Rawlings' Life Agrees to a One-on-One Interview."

His cheeks paled as the blood drained from his face.

"What's the matter?"

Tony heard the concern in Tom's voice. Although their relationship wasn't just that of business, Tony didn't feel like sharing. Prying his eyes away from the article in his tightening grip, Tony forced himself to make eye contact with his longtime friend. "I..." he hesitated. "I-I need a minute. I'll call you when I'm ready to get started."

"Are you sure? Is there something I can—"

"A minute—now," Tony cut him off. It wasn't the volume of his voice that demanded action; it was the authority.

Tom nodded and headed for the door. Within seconds, Tony was alone with the press release that Shelly had tried so desperately to share.

He scanned the pages. Words and phrases jumped out from each paragraph: *Since May of 2010—Anthony's special woman—she agreed to sit down—freelance writer—Meredith Banks—Claire Nichols—* Tony's blood boiled. The tips of his fingers blanched and lost feeling as his grip upon the helpless pages intensified.

More scanning: *long-time friendship is why Claire finally agreed to sit down and discuss her relationship with one of the world's top bachelors.*

Slowly his knees buckled and Tony's tall, muscular body perched on the edge of his large leather chair. He continued reading: *Anthony Rawlings has long been seen as a wonderful catch for that one deserving woman. He dated such women as supermodel Cynthia Simmons and recording artist Julia Owens. However, none of his previous relationships lasted long. That is until now, now that Rawlings and Nichols have been together. These two were first seen together in late May (see picture) at the Quad City Symphony not far from the large wooded estate of Anthony Rawlings. And since that time, they have been spotted by curious onlookers at various charity events, as well as taking on two of the nation's biggest cities, New York (see picture) and Chicago (see picture).*

Intermittently, he flipped back and forth between the pages and the photos of Claire with him. With each word and each picture his vision blurred. Red seeped from every direction, threatening to cover everything in its wake. The pages, his office—hell, his life were all dripping in red.

Such basic rules—*how could Claire have been so stupid as to break the most basic of his rules?* It wasn't like he demanded that much from her.

There was still more article to read, but Tony's eyes couldn't focus. He envisioned Claire the other night at dinner in Chicago. He remembered the dress—it was tan and had sequins, even her jacket had sequins. They caught his attention because of the way they reflected the lights as they walked along the street from Trump Tower to the Cadillac Palace Theater.

Refocusing on the story, he saw the dress—it was in a picture of her with him—on the page before him, prepared for the world to see. *Privacy! Why was that so fuck'n hard to ask?* It wasn't just the damn reporters taking their picture. No, that happened all the time. This was betrayal. *This was disloyalty—insubordination!*

Tony tried to reason. The other day at the barbeque, he'd jumped to conclusions. *Could this be another misunderstanding?* He looked at his watch—2:37 PM, East Coast time. He could be home before 6:00 PM.

He quickly folded the pages and placed them in the inside pocket of his jacket. Next, he dialed the phone on his desk. "Tom, I have to fly immediately back to Iowa."

Tom was understandably shocked. They hadn't reached any resolution on their deal, and they had hundreds of millions of dollars at stake. Tony wouldn't give Tom specifics—only that something had happened back in Iowa, and he needed to be there. Tom assured his boss and his friend that he'd work diligently to keep the deal afloat.

Less than forty minutes later, Tony was airborne and headed west. The three-hour flight gave him ample opportunity to read and reread the article. Each time something new latched onto his consciousness:

Why Claire? What makes her the woman for a man like Anthony Rawlings?—She didn't deny living in the Iowa City area—Claire and Anthony enjoyed the performance of "Wicked."—Ms. Nichols spent the better part of the day enjoying all the comforts money could buy at one of the most exclusive day spas in Chicago—shopping at such stores as Saks Fifth Avenue, Anne Fontaine, Cartier, Giorgio Armani, and Louis Vuitton—Ms. Claire Nichols was ushered to the eighty-ninth floor of Trump Tower, the private city dwelling belonging to none other than Mr. Anthony Rawlings.

By the time the plane touched down in Iowa City, Tony knew he'd need to print another copy of the press release for Claire. The one in his hand was nearly shredded by the fervor of his grasp. He hadn't been willing to let it leave his hand the entire flight.

Each time he told himself to be reasonable, Tony remembered Claire sitting at the dining room table a month ago, pledging her loyalty. He hadn't asked for it. First, because he rarely *asked,* but more importantly, he never assumed he'd get it; nevertheless, on that evening after he'd returned from Europe, she'd offered it.

At the time, he questioned her motivation. After all, they'd just been through an *episode,* a *glitch* of sorts, and Claire had emerged stronger and more compliant than ever—a very appealing combination. He remembered thinking that perhaps *glitches* were an advantageous element in producing the woman he was creating.

That night in the dining room she'd volunteered, "Your absence was advantageous on many counts." He remembered staring at her, stunned by her candor and unsure of where she was going. Finally, she broke the looming silence. "I believe it helped me recognize I owe you much, not just the money to repay my debt, but the confidence you've shown in me."

He watched for signs of manipulation, yet she never faltered.

She had continued, "The confidence to trust me with your intimate beliefs..." She added, "I will not betray that confidence."

Tony remembered allowing the silence to prevail as food came and the staff went. Once they were again alone, he replied, "Claire, if you're sincere, then you never cease to amaze me. If, however, you're playing me, you will regret it." Anthony Rawlings wouldn't be a successful businessman if he couldn't read people, yet as much as he tried to see Claire's deception—he couldn't.

As Tony entered the front door of his estate, he realized his own mistake. It wasn't that he *couldn't* see Claire's deception. It was that he *wouldn't*. He wanted to trust her—hell, for the last month or more, he'd wanted to do more than that. He'd wanted to—dare he admit— have feelings. Now it was clear; Catherine was right: Claire had fuck'n played him!!!

Tony's body trembled with the revelation as he walked toward his office. He needed to print a readable copy of the press release before he confronted Claire. He was done being a push-over. Forget her resolve and bravado. Screw her green eyes, soft skin, and sexy smile.

He brought Claire Nichols to Iowa for one reason—she had a debt to pay. Not the goddamn money. Tony didn't give a rat's ass about $215,000. No, Claire Nichols was the proverbial sacrificial lamb for the entire line of Nichols descendants—a child of a child. The vendetta rang in Tony's head. He'd heard it over and over for twenty years. *So what if he'd extracted some pleasure from her consequence?* That was acceptable; however, her blatant disregard for his rules, her insubordination and disloyalty, were intolerable.

The ridiculous idea running through his mind these past few weeks, that there was anything more between them than business, would end today. Tony would stay strong and deliver the consequences Claire deserved.

When Tony initially entered Claire's suite, he knew his mission: confront her about the interview, entertain the idea of a misconception—at least superficially, and deliver the appropriate punishment. It was a solid plan; however, that was a long time ago. As he sat in the chair near Claire's sofa and minutes turned to hours and hours passed like days, Tony's restraint evaporated. With each tick of the clock, his body stiffened and the red colored his vision.

Three hours! He'd been waiting in her suite for three fuck'n hours!

Catherine told him that Claire had gone to her lake for the day. Tony glanced toward the windows, as darkness fell over the land and enveloped her suite. He told himself, *the damn day is done!*

During the entire three hours that he'd been there, Tony hadn't moved or turned on a light. Truly, he thought it was interesting how well his eyes adjusted. Never before could he remember experiencing each moment of diminishing illumination. As the darkness prevailed, the crimson hue grew.

He worked to contain the fury in his chest and soul. It had been years since he'd experienced this depth of rage. Honestly, he hadn't moved because he feared if he did, he'd break something or some things. That's what used to happen when he was younger. He would break an object or punch a wall. There was one time at Blaire Academy when he punched another kid. The kid deserved it. He had said something about Tony's grandmother. The damn teachers broke it up and no one was seriously hurt; nevertheless, his grandfather didn't care about the why. He warned Anton to never let it happen again, and he hadn't. It was surprisingly easy—remain detached. That was how he could buy companies and fire a roomful of people. They weren't people: they were marks on a ledger.

Initially, this technique worked with Claire, but with each day she'd become more than that. Now, in the quiet suite, with time standing still, his thoughts ran together: *He'd allowed her to become more than that—more than just a Nichols! He'd trusted her—hell, he sent her to the spa, allowed her to shop, and even allowed her to remain in Chicago without him. For what? So that she could spit in his face? So that she could publicly discuss their relationship? What else had she told Meredith Banks? Maybe she had the whole thing planned. Of course, it was her plan to get away from him.*

That was probably it... she arranged it from the spa—hell, he never thought about her using a phone from the spa, or maybe she used a pay phone? He'd supplied her with enough cash. What if she bought one of those disposable phones? The release said Claire and

Meredith were sorority sisters. Claire probably contacted her for this purpose!

There were so many possibilities of how she'd betrayed him. It was true—he didn't know the exact mode, but he knew the final result. The papers were lying on her table—the black and white evidence of her deceit! She'd never meant a word of what she said that day in the dining room. The whole damn speech about trust was a sham, and he was a goddamn fool for falling for it.

Tony's train of thought came to a screeching halt as the sound of the opening door filled the otherwise silent suite. While the moonlight pooled in rectangles on the soft carpet, Tony stepped into the dark shadows and neared the woman who'd consumed his thoughts for the last eight hours—no, for years!

Before she could turn on the light, he stepped behind her. With the redness nearly beyond penetration, her presence and her scent fueled the fury and pain within him. He wrapped his arm around her throat while pulling her ponytail with his other hand. Nearing his lips to her ear, he attempted speech through gritted teeth. "Where the fuck have you been?"

Tony heard the desperation in his voice as it filled the dark room. That desperation poured more crimson onto the fire of his rage. No damn woman, especially a *Nichols*, would have this much control over him!

She didn't speak!

He spun her around—he wanted to see her face, see her lying eyes. Gripping her shoulders, he questioned her again. "I asked you a question. Where the fuck have you been?"

"Tony," she gasped. "I didn't think you were coming home until tomorrow."

His patience expired hours ago. He wanted answers and he wanted them now. He slapped her cheek. *Damn her, why wasn't she apologizing for her disloyalty? Why wasn't she answering his fuck'n question?* "I have asked you a question twice. I will not ask again."

His palm stung as it once again connected with her cheek and temple. The red behind his eyes obscured the growing physical evidence of his more forceful contact. Truly, he didn't even see the tears as they began to fall from her pleading eyes.

"Tony, please stop. I was hiking in the woods."

Letting go of her shoulders, he shoved her onto the sofa and followed. Leaning over her petite body, his words sounded too desperate for his own ears. "Do you expect me to believe you were in the woods until this time of night?"

"I was in the woods"—*lies*— "The sun was setting"—*bullshit*— "It was so beautiful."

He couldn't take it anymore! He wanted the truth! "Shut the fuck up! You were out there because you knew I was coming home, and you didn't want to face me after what you did!"

"I don't know what you mean. You told me you were coming home on Saturday—this is still Friday. I haven't done anything."

She was lying. He struck out again. Claire reached for her cheek as she tried to hide her face. He pulled her chin toward him; she wasn't looking away! His breath bathed her tear-drenched face. "Liar!"

He searched her eyes. *Why weren't they contrite or smug? She'd successfully humiliated him, broken his rules—why wasn't she assuming credit for her deceit?*

Tony stepped away. He couldn't look at her expression another minute. Inhaling deeply, he pushed the sound of her sobs from his ears and stepped toward the light switch. While the light filled the suite, Tony concentrated on inhaling and exhaling as he walked toward the table. *Maybe if she read the release she'd accept responsibility.*

The sound of her whimpering on the sofa tempered the red, causing it to wane, but when the tips of his fingers touched the pages of the news release, the crimson violently resurged through his veins. He didn't want the red to be so intense—if he didn't keep it down, he knew it had the ability to control him. Tony didn't want to give in to it, but he sure as hell wasn't giving that control to Claire. His neck stiffened. He refused to proceed lightly; it was his choice. Claire's damn emotions weren't going to deter his quest for truth. Stepping toward her, he held out the pages and steadied his voice. "Then tell me—tell me how this is a misunderstanding." The pages in his hand shook. Despite his best effort, his words came out too close together. "I jumped to conclusions last time. Tell me how I'm doing that now."

Tony wondered why he was giving her the chance to talk her way out. Maybe he wanted to push that bravado. *Would she try to talk her way out of this?* Most people would know better—they would accept the consequences and leave him alone. *Should he even allow it?*

Claire's voice interrupted his internal debate. "Tony, I'm sorry. I really don't know what you are talking about."

He threw the pages toward her and watched as they scattered on the floor near her feet. He didn't move; instead he stared and watched as Claire moved to the floor. Tony knew every word—hell, he'd read it fifty times. He watched as she fumbled with the pages, and her breathing became ragged.

"Tony, oh my God, I did *not* agree to an interview."

He was once again beside her. *What kind of pull did she have on him?* He pointed to the picture. "So you're telling me that the picture of you talking to this woman is a print shop fabrication and this is a colossal misunderstanding?"

"It is me, but—"

He seized her shoulders, lifted her from the floor, and pinned her against a wall. The falling picture and fear in her eyes didn't register.

Her voice begged for understanding. "I wasn't giving an interview."

She was lying to him! He slapped her again! If he had to, he'd force the truth out of her. He leaned down until their noses almost touched. *Would she have the audacity to look him in the eye and continue lying?* "Then what in the hell were you doing?" He shook her again. "Claire, I trusted you! You told me I could trust you, and I believed you. I sent you to a spa day. This is how you thank me? This is how you repay me? By breaking all my rules? By public failure?"

Abruptly, he released her shoulders. He wasn't going there. He refused to reveal how betrayed he felt. That would give her too much power. *She didn't have the power, he did.* And he would prove it!

When he turned around, Claire was scurrying to pick up the papers. The sight of her face finally registered: it was red and blotchy, yet her voice fought for steadiness. "What is this?"

Fine—he could be steady too. "It's an exclusive Internet release of an upcoming story. It'll run simultaneously in *People* and *Rolling Stone*."

In an effort to control the emotions he didn't want to feel, he stepped away, went to the bookshelf, picked up a book, and threw it into the fireplace. The release served as a small vent. After a deep inhale, he answered, "Shelly, my publicist, found it today and immediately forwarded me a copy. I flew home as soon as I could."

While she read, Tony walked to the sofa, sat, and watched. The pages in her hand trembled as tears fell onto the printed words. *What the hell did she think—that he wouldn't find out? That he wouldn't know she'd betrayed his trust?*

"Tony, I did go to school with Meredith. She did come up to me the other day and start talking. I didn't know she was a reporter. I wasn't giving an interview. I didn't say anything about you." She cried, "Your name was never mentioned!"

Tony didn't speak; instead, he nodded toward the pages. Claire continued reading. When it appeared as though she were finally done, she didn't move. She didn't look up, or speak—or anything. Tony waited. The only sound in the suite was that of their breathing. Tony's was getting louder while Claire's became shallower. Eventually, she laid the pages on the carpet and kept her eyes downcast.

His fury had ebbed. On much steadier legs, he walked toward her. "Appearances, Claire. How many times have I told you? Appearances mean everything. There's a picture, right here, of you sitting with her, the author. It doesn't matter if what she writes is accurate. It's believable because she's seen talking to you."

He wasn't yelling; he'd regained some control, yet the aura of rage remained. Claire still didn't look up. He wanted to see her face; instead, all that he could see was the top of her head. Some of her hair had come loose from the ponytail and hung in front of her eyes. "Get up," he ordered.

She didn't move—not a flinch.

His volume increased. "Claire, get up!"

Still looking at the carpet she begged, "P-please, Tony, I-I'm so sorry."

He reached for her arm, lifted her, and said, "The entire way home I was praying that somehow this was another misunderstanding. You wouldn't do this, not after I put my trust in you, but I knew if it wasn't a misunderstanding, there had to be consequences. There had to be punishment for this blatant disregard for the most fundamental of rules."

Claire wouldn't look at his eyes. When he reached for her chin, she moved away from his touch. The red returned and filled every molecule of the suite. *How dare she pull away from him!* He moved again, not to lift her chin, but to strike her face. If she were going to pull away, he'd give her something to pull away from. His hand caught her pearl necklace, and Tony watched as the small pearl charm flew across the room.

He would do more than punish her physically for her betrayal. Next time, she would remember to follow his rules. Tony emphasized his control over her liberties as he continued, "I believe some time away from people, some time alone in your suite, will help you remember who and who not to talk to."

The betrayal combined with the fear in her eyes was too much. She was speaking, but he couldn't hear. She was fighting him or protecting herself. Tony wasn't sure anymore. Nothing made sense.

It was like the boy at the Academy—only multiplied. It wasn't right, but he couldn't stop. Claire's behavior caused him pain. At the moment, the only thing he could think to do was return the favor.

How long did he hurt her? Tony truly didn't know. It wasn't until she stopped fighting, stopped begging, and stopped moving, that the red disappeared.

When it did, the only thing that remained was Claire.

"Claire, get up." She didn't move. "Claire?" Tony reached for her shoulder as she lay upon the floor. Blood trickled from her lip, and her face was beginning to bruise.

Tony fell to his knees and shook her. She still didn't respond. He tried again. This time his touch was soft and gentle. He wanted to shake her harder and wake her from this sleep, but he couldn't. The rage and fury, which seconds earlier had consumed his entire being, faded into nothingness. Momentarily, his soul felt empty. Then, slowly, the void within his chest filled. It filled with fear—a fear like he'd never known.

"Oh, my God, what have I done?" he murmured. Reaching for her pulse, he said a prayer. Tony really wasn't sure to whom, but at that moment he knew the thing he wanted more than anything else in the entire world was for her to live. Not because he didn't deserve to pay for what he'd done. He prayed for her to live, because Claire didn't deserve to die or to suffer as he'd made her suffer. "Please, don't be dead. Oh God, help... Claire... please, please, let her wake up..."

Before his fingers found her pulse, the suite door opened.

"What have you done?"

His eyes met Catherine's, but words failed him.

She knelt beside Claire and pushed Tony's hand away. Finally, she said what he'd prayed to hear. "She has a pulse." Catherine stood. Her stance straightened as her expression turned stoic. There was no understanding or compassion, only determination in her steel-gray eyes as she looked down at him. "Anton, you need to think straight. What are we going to do?"

Tony didn't answer. His mind couldn't process. *Did Catherine actually think he wanted this to happen? Had that ever been his desire?* Seeing Claire's crumpled body, he couldn't remember what they'd wanted or planned. Instead of answering, he scooped her petite, unconscious frame into his arms and carried her to her bed. Catherine exhaled audibly, followed, and pulled back the blankets. Tony gently laid Claire upon the soft mattress and watched as she lay still, exactly as he placed her. Sitting next to her, his shoulders heaved as his head fell to her chest. Catherine waited.

After a deep breath, Tony sat straight, turned toward Catherine, and said, "Call 911. She needs medical care."

"No! You can't do that. Don't you know what will happen to you?"

Slowly, he covered Claire's body with the blankets and tenderly placed her hands above the covers. Taking her hand in his, he momentarily caressed her soft skin with his thumb. Next, he smoothed her disheveled hair away from her battered face and gently kissed her forehead. His thoughts moved much slower than before, as if all his adrenaline were gone. Even his words sounded far away. "She looks like she's sleeping." He looked to Catherine for confirmation. "That's it, isn't it? She's sleeping?"

"We can take care of her, like I took care of—"

"No," he interrupted. His determination was back. "She needs a doctor."

Catherine moved near Claire's head and touched her cheek. This situation wasn't negotiable; he wouldn't compromise. After a moment of obvious internal debate, Tony saw Catherine's shoulders droop and heard the slightest hint of compassion. "Then we need a story. You helped me. I'm here to help you."

"Well, there's a difference. When she gets better, she'll be able to tell someone the truth. Unlike before, *they* never got that chance." Tony reached for his cell phone.

Before he could dial, Catherine touched his arm. Her voice was calm and reassuring. "Listen to me and listen carefully. Claire went for a walk. The ground was wet; she slipped; she didn't come home. I called and told you. We were worried. You rushed home. You went looking for her and found her—like this. Maybe someone else was out there?"

Tony looked around the suite. It was as if he were looking at the path of a tornado. *How did this all happen?* The picture that usually hung near the fireplace was lying on the carpet. The pages of the news release were scattered near the sofa. Shaking his head, he replied, "No, I deserve whatever she tells the authorities."

"*If* she's able to tell them."

"She will be. I'll spare no expense. We'll get her anything she needs. One day, she'll have the opportunity to send me away for this."

"And maybe she won't. Why confess now? Let's see what happens first."

Tony caressed Claire's right cheek; the left one was turning a darker shade of purple by the minute. "I need to get her help. She didn't deserve this."

"Then call Dr. Leonard. If you call 911, the police will come. Just call him directly."

Tony nodded. Telling the authorities would be Claire's decision. He needed to get her well enough to do it. Searching his contacts, he found the doctor's number. Moments later he heard a voice on Dr. Leonard's private line. "Hello, Dr. Leonard, this is Anthony Rawlings. I need you to come to my estate immediately. There's been a terrible *accident...*"

Chapter 8

The days and weeks that followed
—September 2010

(Consequences—Chapter 21)

———◆———

You usually have to wait for that
which is worth waiting for.
—Craig Bruce

TONY STROKED THE side of Claire's arm as he mindlessly listened to the conversation behind him. Dr. Leonard spoke softly. "Ms. London, I'm obligated to call the authorities."

"Doctor, Mr. Rawlings has already contacted the Iowa City police department. They currently have officers combing the grounds for signs of the assailant—if there was one. We don't know for sure what happened."

He cleared his throat. "Then Mr. Rawlings won't mind if I speak with them, too?"

"You'll need to discuss that with him. However, I don't believe now is a good time. As you can see, Mr. Rawlings is very distraught over Ms. Nichols' condition."

"Yes, I see that."

"Can you tell me again what you believe happened?" Dr. Leonard inquired.

"We don't know. Nothing like this has ever happened before. Ms. Nichols likes to go for walks in the woods—she does it frequently. When she didn't return, I became worried and called..."

Tony blocked out their voices; he knew each word before Catherine said it. He'd told the same story multiple times. After summoning Dr. Leonard, he'd called the police. While the doctor assessed Claire, two seasoned officers arrived at the door and took Tony's statement. He met with them in his office and gave them his statement: got home—woods—found her—unsure. They'd worked for ICPD for years, were well aware of Anthony Rawlings, and unquestioningly took Tony's statement at face value. When they asked to speak to Claire, Tony explained that she was with the doctor and unconscious. They thanked him for his time, shut their notepads, and promised to comb the grounds for clues. Tony explained that his security team was already searching, but the ICPD was more than welcome to join the hunt. There were probably more footprints in the back woods than there'd been in a decade.

Not surprisingly, nothing was found; however, each time the contrived story was retold, the fiction became more plausible. At some point, even part of Tony began to believe it—until he looked at Claire.

The police said that they'd do another search of the grounds once it was light. As Tony peered toward the heavy drapes, he realized that despite the longest day of his life, the sun had yet to rise—but he knew it would. That happened every morning. What ate at him—nagged at the depths of his soul—was Claire. Would she rise? It had been over six hours since her *accident*, and Dr. Leonard remained evasive at best, regarding her diagnosis. Even after all of his tests and examination, she remained the same—suspended in time. The only change was her appearance. The areas on her face and body that had at one time been red were darkening and swelling—distorting her facial features in a way that Tony would never be able to forget.

After Dr. Leonard's initial examination, he'd said that Claire's vitals were strong, but he wanted to run more tests. He recommended an MRI and other procedures that had acronyms instead of names. Tony agreed to any test or any treatment that could be done on the estate. He refused to move her to a hospital, but instead offered any amount of money to bring the hospital to her.

Although that apparently couldn't include an MRI, it did include portable ultrasound and x-ray machines. The images those machines generated confirmed that a few of Claire's ribs were broken. The doctor suspected that she also suffered a concussion, but without all the tests, he couldn't confirm that diagnosis. A large needle was inserted and held in place on Claire's left arm delivering a combination of fluids and pain medication. Even though she appeared blissfully asleep, Dr. Leonard said that if she were conscious, she'd be in a lot of pain. The doctor warned repeatedly about brain swelling—something about the brain being trapped within the skull and unable to heal. He mentioned the possibility of long-term damage, side effects, possible death. Tony listened, he did. For someone who could retain figures and information, what the doctor was telling him proved too overwhelming. He couldn't retain the prognosis if he wanted to—and he didn't. It wasn't possible. Just seven hours ago, she'd been fine.

Repeatedly, Tony cursed the bastard or circumstance that did this to his *companion*.

⸻ ◆ ⸻

TONY'S SHOULDERS ACHED and his head throbbed as his eyes opened and his blurry world began to focus. It took a few seconds for reality to register—but when it did, it hit with a vengeance. Sometime after 4:00

AM, he'd fallen asleep with his head on the side of Claire's mattress and his hand over her arm. She wasn't sleeping in their bed. No, Dr. Leonard had done as Tony wished and brought the hospital to her. That included a motorized hospital bed and monitors that beeped. Tony scanned her petite frame looking for any sign of movement: there was none. She lay exactly as she had before he'd fallen asleep.

Wisps of sunlight reddened the outside sky and still Tony had yet to take any calls from Tom or Tim, or anyone at Rawlings Industries. At the moment, he wasn't even sure what he'd done with his cell phone. The big deal in New York seemed like a million years ago. He no longer cared if it worked out or if it didn't. All that time and all that money suddenly seemed inconsequential. Tony didn't care about anything other than seeing Claire's eyes open. Once, late last night, when they were alone, he lifted one of her eyelids to try to see the green, but he couldn't. He lifted the lid, but all he saw was white, and it was full of red. The other lid he didn't dare touch. It was swollen and dark, as was the area surrounding it.

Tony's stomach lurched at the sight of her bruises as they colored and swelled. He convinced himself to look beyond her exterior and see the real Claire underneath. With time, he no longer saw the bandages or the discoloration. When Tony looked at the woman before him, he saw the vivacious, strong-willed woman whom he loved to bait. He saw the woman who could look him in the eye when most would turn away. He saw the beautiful blonde highlights and the emerald-green eyes. He saw the refined woman he'd created—the one who fit perfectly on his arm at social gatherings and perfectly beneath him on a soft mattress. He imagined the fire—he wanted the fire. The images gave him a false sense of hope as the blissfulness of sleep once again took him to a better place.

The next time Tony woke, it was due to Catherine's hand on his shoulder. "Anton, Dr. Leonard will be in here in a few minutes. Do you want me to sit with her while you clean up?"

Tony glanced at his watch—after 8:00 AM. The morning sun streamed across Claire's makeshift bed and accentuated the bruises he didn't want to see. It wasn't just her face: her arms were discolored too. It didn't take a forensic pathologist to recognize that one bruise on her left arm resembled a handprint.

Where had he been for the last few hours? He'd awakened once, but then he began remembering and scenes floated in and out. He remembered Claire describing the lake on his property. He remembered her excitement and joy. It was almost contagious as her eyes and expression glowed. Maybe he could take her there? Maybe then she'd wake?

No, she'd been there—yesterday.

Tony squeezed Claire's hand. *How could that have only been yesterday?* Her cold unresponsive skin caused the bile in his empty stomach to bubble and surge upward. He nodded his approval to Catherine and moved quickly to Claire's bathroom. He had just enough time to close the door before he was headfirst into the toilet. It wasn't like he'd eaten recently, yet his memories wouldn't give him a reprieve.

Claire had been to her lake. That's where she was—while he was in her suite. She was there, among the flowers and water and beach and trees and all of the things she talked about. She wasn't plotting to leave him. She wasn't basking in some sense of betrayal. No, she was finding solace like only she could. She'd tried to tell him, tried to explain—and what had he done?

His stomach heaved again and again. It was as if his body were trying to expel a part of himself—a part that was deep inside and needed to be gone, a part that Claire didn't deserve.

With a pounding in his temples like he'd never before known,

Tony laid his head on the cool porcelain and closed his eyes. Time passed—he didn't know much, but eventually voices could be heard from beyond his cloud. Painstakingly, he rose and walked to Claire's shower. Turning on the water, he disrobed. As the steam filled the bathroom, he stepped under the scalding spray. Liquid fire assaulted his skin. He didn't turn down the temperature. No, Tony wanted the pain—he needed it, he deserved it. When his body adapted, he turned the temperature up. It wasn't until he heard the knock at the door that he even considered the amount of time he'd stood helplessly accepting the spray's punishment.

Stepping from the glass enclosure, he realized he'd not considered fresh clothes. It was then he heard the knock again accompanied by a voice. "Anton, I brought you some clothes. Dr. Leonard went downstairs to eat breakfast. If you're done with your shower, let me give these to you and you can go down and join him. He's finished his most recent examination."

Tony leaned his head against the wall and exhaled. *Thank God he had Catherine. He'd never felt so helpless. Maybe that was how she'd felt at one time; he didn't know. He just knew that if it were not for her, he'd be in a jail cell, or out on bond. Either way, she was his rock and he was so thankful they'd supported one another.*

When he opened the door slightly, he met Catherine's gaze. "Thank you," was all he could manage.

She didn't respond, other than to nod. It was enough. He couldn't have taken her gloating nor her telling him that he'd let the whole thing with Claire get out of hand. He knew that. He needed Catherine's support, and seeing her steady steel expression, that was exactly what she offered.

Wiping the steam from Claire's mirror, Tony's reflection peered back at him. The unfamiliar image with reddened skin, cheeks and chin covered by a day's beard growth, and tired eyes, wasn't what taunted him. It was the tremendous invisible weight crushing his shoulders. The anxiety surrounding Claire's recovery was more than psychological. It was physical, making standing difficult as his knees flexed. For a moment, Tony laid his head on the vanity and debated if he could go on. Then he remembered Claire's fight—the fire he longed to see. The fire he knew was somewhere inside of her. If she could fight to get through this—no, as she fought to get through this—so would he. She needed him to be strong, needed him to be there for her—to help her. He wouldn't let her down, not again. After a few minutes, Tony was down in the dining room, drinking a much-needed cup of coffee, and listening to Dr. Leonard.

Over the next days, Dr. Leonard moved onto the estate. Catherine gave him a bedroom near Claire's, which served as his makeshift office. He told most of his staff that he'd taken an unexpected leave to look after an ailing family member, and another private practitioner graciously agreed to see his patients. Only one member of his staff was enlightened to his true endeavor. She was his trusted nurse and assistant. Both medical professionals agreed to total confidentiality; however, Dr. Leonard maintained his legal responsibilities. Although he didn't come out and say it, Tony knew exactly what he meant: if he could prove that Claire had been harmed by someone on the estate, he would report it.

Dr. Leonard's nurse didn't stay at the estate, but she came and went with some frequency, bringing Dr. Leonard whatever he wanted from his office or from the hospital. She also assisted him with much of Claire's care. She changed IV bags, gave medication, moved Claire so that she didn't stay in one position too long, gave her bed baths, and changed her gown. At first, Dr. Leonard insisted on a hospital gown: it was easier access for his examinations, but Tony hated the sight of it. He immediately sent for nightgowns that buttoned up the front with long sleeves. Dr. Leonard could still have access for his exams, but

Claire didn't look as much like a patient.

Even without the MRI, the doctor concluded that Claire's initial unconsciousness was due to a blow to her head. There was no way of knowing the cause of that blow, only that evidence suggested that it had occurred. He immediately put her on additional medication to reduce swelling of her brain. Her medication also included something to keep her sedated. The doctor explained that it was for the best.

Day after day, either Tony or Catherine sat by her side. They only left the room when Dr. Leonard or his nurse insisted. Even then, it was only for a short duration. The doctor couldn't confirm that Claire could hear the world around her; nevertheless, Tony talked as much as he could. Everything felt wrong. Usually the suite was filled with the sound of Claire's voice, and Tony found the silence deafening. Often he'd ask her to wake. "Claire, talk to us. Open your eyes." Sometimes he'd read—usually things related to Rawlings Industries—but he continued to speak. The only time Tony allowed the blanket of quiet to cover the room was at night. He no longer slept with his head on her bed; instead, he had a large recliner brought to her bedside and slept there.

For over a week, Tony relinquished full control of Rawlings Industries to his vice president, Tim. Tony asked Patricia to not contact him, unless it was a dire emergency. He received emails, and those, too, he'd read aloud. That was how he'd learned that the New York negotiations had finally resulted in a deal. Truthfully, he wasn't happy. It was that *deal* that took him out of Chicago; it was that *deal* that left Claire alone. It was that *deal* that Tony held responsible for the condition of the woman before him. Despite years of work and hundreds of thousands of dollars, Tony emailed Tim and told him to sell off the investment and securities firm and to do it as soon as possible. He didn't care what happened to the damn employees, their pensions, their benefits, or anything else. Anthony Rawlings wanted the damn firm out from under the Rawlings umbrella.

As time passed, Claire's bruises began to fade. Tony hoped and prayed that if the swelling on the outside was decreasing, that meant that the swelling on the inside was too. Claire's IV now contained some kind of nutritional supplement. In essence, the nurse explained, Claire was being fed from the tube in her arm, and Tony hated it. Claire wasn't that big to begin with; yet each day she seemed to shrink behind the nightgown and blankets. Multiple times a day he'd move her arms and legs as the nurse taught him to do. Each time he lifted her limbs, they felt lighter in his grasp. It was also during those times that he saw her otherwise covered bruises. The areas that used to be red first faded to blue/purple, and were turning green and yellow. Each time he was faced with these markings, Tony made himself see beyond the green discolorations. The only green he wanted to see was behind her lids.

Although, Dr. Leonard warned that she might not ever wake, Tony refused to believe that. Claire's eyes would open and when they did, she'd be coherent. The possible traumatic brain injury that the nurse discussed was nonsense. Claire was too strong for that.

IT TOOK ALMOST two weeks, but finally it happened. Slowly, Dr. Leonard had discontinued the medicine to keep Claire from waking. Since that time, there had been small signs of movement. Sometimes her lids fluttered or her fingers twitched, but then one afternoon with both Catherine and Tony present, her eyes opened and she looked right at Tony. He could hardly speak through his relief. Finally, he found his voice. "Claire, are you awake?"

Catherine must have heard the change in his voice, because immediately she was at the other side of Claire's bed. "Ms. Claire, please come back to us."

Tony spoke fast. "She opened her eyes. I saw it—just a second ago." He reached for her hand—it was still so cold. "Claire, can you hear me?" He continued speaking to Catherine, "Go get the doctor. He's getting something to eat in the kitchen. Let him know she's finally waking." With a different tone, one of desperation and affection, he pleaded, "Claire, please open your eyes."

She obeyed, just as he'd taught her to do, but when she did, she immediately squinted. He jumped up and shut the heavy drapes. With only the light from the bedside stand, the colors within the suite muted, making her bruises less visible. Tony smiled as tenderly as he could and prayed that she would be able to talk. He didn't want to think about the nurse's warnings. Fighting back those thoughts, he lifted her hand and said, "It was too bright in here. I closed the drapes for you. Is that better?"

Her mouth moved, but nothing came out. His chest tightened as a tear fell from her once again closed eyes.

"It's okay, you don't need to talk," he said, trying to reassure her. "Please open your eyes again. It's so good to see your beautiful emerald eyes." Tony didn't know if it was his imagination, but her hand felt warmer. Her eyes opened and moved to the needle taped into the bend of her left arm. He explained, "That's how you've been eating for almost two weeks, and it has some pain medicine too—to make you more comfortable."

Her expression went from uncertainty to—Tony wasn't sure— terror? With her eyes open wide, he tried to reassure her by talking. After all, he'd been doing nothing but talk for over ten days; now he couldn't seem to stop. "Can you remember what happened? You had an accident."

She stared.

He wanted to know she understood. *Did she even know who he was? What was she thinking?* He continued, "You had an accident in the woods. When we found you, your jeans and boots were all muddy, and you had multiple injuries. Did you fall? Did you slip? Did someone or something out there hurt you? We've had the woods searched. Nothing was found." He leaned toward her. "Claire, we've been so worried about you."

Catherine and Dr. Leonard rushed into the suite. Dr. Leonard pushed forward, toward his patient. Obviously, he was as concerned as everyone else with her cognitive abilities. So far, Tony didn't know what to think. He only knew she was finally awake. He looked to the doctor and silently mouthed, "I don't know."

"Ms. Nichols, I'm Dr. Leonard. I've been taking care of you since Mr. Rawlings found you in the woods. Can you talk to me?"

Claire lifted her right hand to her throat.

They all smiled; Claire was trying to communicate. The doctor spoke, "Catherine, could you please get Ms. Nichols some water?" When she returned, Dr. Leonard put the straw to Claire's lips and commanded, "Drink slowly; your stomach has been empty for a while."

Claire began to sip.

The doctor turned to Tony. "Mr. Rawlings, as you can imagine, this is a very good sign. Due to the length of time Ms. Nichols was unconscious, I was hesitant to make any predictions. I believe we have just passed an important juncture in her care and with that, my prognosis for her has greatly improved." He removed the straw from her lips.

"Please, that was so good," Claire said. The room went silent. Everyone turned to her.

Tony spoke first, "Claire, thank God. How do you feel?"

"I feel—I feel—tired—and kind of dizzy." Her voice quivered unsteadily.

"Mr. Rawlings, I need to ask you and Catherine to allow Ms. Nichols some privacy while I examine her."

Catherine nodded and stood; however, Tony didn't want to let go of Claire's hand. He could gaze into her eyes forever. "Doctor, I can assure you, there is nothing I haven't seen. I don't believe Claire will mind if I stay."

"Mr. Rawlings, I realize you hired me; however, as a medical doctor, I need to see and speak to Ms. Nichols alone. You'll be welcomed back as soon as we're done." Tony stared at Dr. Leonard. The doctor continued, "Mr. Rawlings, she is *not* related to you. We must allow her some privacy."

Tony knew that the doctor was right. It was that, as he released her hand, Tony had the ominous feeling that he'd never hold it again. All it would take was for Claire to tell Dr. Leonard the truth, and the judgment he'd weeks ago been willing to accept, would be his. For so long, he didn't know if Claire would ever be able to tell the truth. Even now, he wasn't sure if she remembered it, but something about the way she looked at him while they were alone, told him she did remember. He squeezed her hand. "I'm sorry, Doctor," he said to Dr. Leonard. "You're right. It's just that it's been so long since she's been awake. I don't want to leave her." Standing, he continued, "I will; I'll be right outside the door. Please call me when you're finished." He then leaned over, kissed Claire on her forehead, and took one last long gaze into her beautiful green eyes.

Catherine was waiting in the hallway. As soon as he shut the door, she said, "What are you going to do if she tells?"

"What do you mean, what will I do? What choice do I have?"

Their voices were a stage whisper as they walked away from Claire's suite. "You have money. You have a lot of money. That money bought silence once before—it can do it again."

"Dr. Leonard already knows what happened. He's all but told me."

Catherine stood taller. "Anton, think! You aren't thinking straight. You refused to silence Claire—silence Dr. Leonard."

His eyes opened wide. "What the hell are you suggesting?"

Catherine shook her head. "Not that. I'm suggesting *money*. Everyone has his price. Pull up the monitor on your phone and learn what she's saying. Be prepared. For God's sake, do you think your grandfather would have wanted you to come this far to lose everything because of one mistake with a Nichols girl?" She reached for his shoulders. "It was an *accident*. They happen. Stop berating yourself and act like the man Nathaniel knew you could be." She took a deep breath. "Anton, I've seen that man. I know he's there. I've watched him succeed against all odds. Look around you. You did this. You made Nathaniel's fortune and more. You are Anton Rawls/Anthony Rawlings. Don't let this derail everything."

He didn't like what he was hearing, but now that Claire was all right, now that he knew she would survive, it was easier to take a step back. It was an *accident*. They'd been working too long and had too many triumphs to let it all unravel. He nodded and pulled the phone from his pocket. As he began to bring up the app, he thought about money. *How much would this cost him? Catherine's accident cost him a substantial payment each year. If he could pay for her mistake, he could pay for his own.* Dr. Leonard did seem like a respectable doctor; nevertheless, money had enticed him to step away from his own practice for two weeks—if it could do that, the possibilities were limitless.

The screen was small, yet when he held it out, both he and Catherine could see and hear. Claire was speaking, "...I'm very tired and my memories are fuzzy."

"It's all right," Dr. Leonard said. "Let me put your bed back." He pushed the button to recline the bed and continued to inquire. "Now, please, what do you remember?"

"Doctor, I'm going to get sick." Claire sat up with a wince. The doctor grabbed a basin, and the water Claire had drunk came back up.

Tony felt Catherine's hand on his shoulder.

"Miss Nichols, it's okay. It's normal—your stomach has been empty for too long. Ms. Nichols, your pain medicine has started to wear off. I'll get you some more, but I want you to be thinking straight. Please tell me what happened."

Claire was now trembling and crying. Tony wanted to go back in the room. "I need to stop this. She isn't strong enough right now. Why can't he see that? He can do this another time."

"He can," Catherine said. "That's why he's pushing. He's hoping to catch her at her weakest."

Catherine's words burned deep. She was right. Dr. Leonard came across as nice and trustworthy, but here was evidence of how methodical and dubious he truly was. Tony refocused on his screen. The doctor gave Claire more water but instructed her to only rinse and spit into the basin. She began to speak, "I went for a walk in the woods... I like the woods... it rained the day before... and the ground was slippery in some spots... I made it into the woods fine... but I let it get dark... I watched the sun set... I remember it being crimson and beautiful." She laid her head back on the pillow and closed her eyes.

"Please continue, Ms. Nichols."

"So it was dark by the time I headed back to the house. I remember getting to the clearing—which is about forty-five minutes from here. The sun... I mean, the moon... was bright... I tried to get back... Catherine had dinner waiting for me." Her words slowed and slurred.

Tony started to move and Catherine touched his arm. "It's too late," she whispered.

He nodded as his heart pounded rapidly in his chest. Dr. Leonard spoke softly. "Ms. Nichols, did you make it back to the house?"

"I don't remember." Claire's voice became stronger. "I remember slipping in the mud. There were roots and limbs. It was very dark under the trees. After that, I just don't know."

"Please know, Ms. Nichols, anything you disclose to me is said in confidence. I'm bound by complete patient-doctor confidentiality."

"Doctor, I'm not sure what you're asking me or what you're implying, but I can't remember what happened that night. Perhaps I hit my head?" Her eyes were open and brimming with tears. "Please, may I rest?"

The look of surprise that Tony saw on Catherine's face was surely a reflection of his own. For another moment, they both stood in silence.

"Well then," Catherine finally said, "congratulations, you did it. I doubted you, but you did it."

Tony put his phone in his pocket and fell against the corridor wall. "*We* did."

Just then the door to the suite opened. "Mr. Rawlings, Ms. Nichols is very tired, but you're welcome to come back in. Let me explain my findings..."

Chapter 9

Will you—Can I?—November 2010

(Consequences—Chapter 24)

———————◆———————

**Manipulation, fueled with good intent,
can be a blessing. But when used wickedly, it is the
beginning of a magician's karmic calamity.**
—T.F. Hodge

TONY HAD BEEN mulling the idea over and over in his head since Claire first woke from her *accident*. At first, it was only a fleeting thought, but then he would remember what it was like to be without Claire, and the idea of making her presence more permanent would seep into his mind. The way he saw it, Claire passed the ultimate test when she followed his rules and kept private information private. She'd had the opportunity to tell Dr. Leonard what truly happened—not just the accident. That would've been the tip of the iceberg—one story would have led to another. Oh, Tony had contingency plans. That's why he purposely created the *gold-digging* persona, but with her injuries, public opinion would've undoubtedly gone in her direction. Tony may have been able to keep it out of the media—he was prepared to pay Dr. Leonard an exorbitant amount of money to maintain his secrets—yet thanks to Claire's obedience, it never went that far. She had the perfect opportunity to expose him, and she didn't.

Starting that day in the hallway, as he listened to her with Dr. Leonard, through her recovery, onto their car ride when he took her to the meadow, confessed his behavior and she responded favorably, Tony began to see that Claire was the woman he wanted in his life. Anthony Rawlings usually got what he wanted. When he carried Claire to his bedroom after their car ride, it was his ultimate invitation. In all the years he'd lived on his estate, he'd never taken a woman to his bedroom. He didn't need to. He could take them to hotels or to their place. On the rare occasion that he brought a woman to the estate, he had plenty of bedrooms. No one, not one other woman, had ever seen his private suite—his ultimate personal space. Claire didn't know that, but Tony did. When he carried her from the car to his room, he opened a part of himself that he'd never shown to anyone else. It was a meaningful gift that she didn't know she'd received.

Months ago, he'd taken a strong young woman and refined her. Tony supposed it was like the process with gold, where excessive heat removes the impurities. In his process, he'd taken Claire into the fire and come away with the perfect companion—wife? Until recently, he'd never imagined marrying—anyone. Until recently, there'd been no one who could handle the job. Claire proved that she could handle it and more. She knew how to appropriately behave in public and in private. She was pleasing to the eye and even more pleasing to be with. Without planning to do so, Tony and Catherine had created the perfect Mrs. Rawlings.

It also seemed that realistically, Tony couldn't hold her prisoner forever. From the beginning, he knew that one day the arrangement would need to end. *What better long-term bind than a wedding ring?* That's what he explained to Catherine, when he told her that he'd finally decided to ask Claire to be his wife. Stoically, Catherine reminded him of the problems that his changes to their plan had already created. He reminded her that all the problems were under control, and assured her that they would remain under control when Claire was no longer a Nichols.

To Tony, that was the best part of his plan. Over the last eight months, he'd successfully removed Claire Nichols from the woman who slept beside him. She was, in actuality, the same woman, but anyone could see, she'd become someone new—from her new even blonder hair and leaner build, to the most important quality—her behavior. The woman who walked away from her job as a bartender at the Red Wing no longer existed. Tony wasn't sure if even Claire realized the transition she'd been through.

The woman he'd created was as close to perfect as he could imagine. He also felt confident that as time passed, if further refinement was necessary, he was more than qualified to facilitate the change. After all, their paradigm was set. He was the teacher and Claire was the student. That wouldn't change once they were married. The real change would be in the eyes of the world: everyone would know that she was his.

Dr. Leonard had been right to ask Tony to leave the room when she woke. He'd said, "She isn't related to you, Mr. Rawlings." That phrase rang over and over in Tony's mind. The doctor had been right. Tony wanted the whole world to know that Claire *did* belong to him. No one would ever question his presence or right to be near her again.

As Eric drove Tony toward his New York City apartment building, Tony anticipated the evening he had planned. Everything was set, except her answer.

In most cases of business, Tony was sure of the answers he'd receive before he received them. With Claire, he wasn't one-hundred-percent sure. He'd debated his proposal. He had a stunning ring from Tiffany and Company, but it was his wording that he couldn't decide on. Over the course of the last eight months, Claire had been allowed very few choices. He wondered how it would be possible to ask her to choose marriage, without actually allowing her to choose. *If he did that, was that what he really wanted?* Her silence with Dr. Leonard was definitely a passed test. If presented with marriage or continued indebtedness, would he know that she truly wanted to marry him? Of course not. The only real test of her true feelings would be to offer her an alternate choice—her freedom.

The prospect made him nervous as hell.

What if she chose freedom? What if she said she wanted to leave him and never look back? Where would she go? Surely, she realized that there was nothing remaining of her previous life. Her apartment, car, and job were gone. She still had her sister. Even that was part of his plan. Claire didn't know that her family was scheduled to join them for Thanksgiving dinner. *What would happen if she decided on freedom?* Without a doubt, she'd need to maintain his rules—private information could still not be divulged. *Could he let her go?*

Tony didn't know.

When he entered the apartment's bedroom, Tony was momentarily mesmerized by the woman at the mirror. Walking behind her, he nuzzled her neck. As his breath bathed her soft, perfumed skin, he said, "Good evening, Claire. I trust you were successful today with your shopping endeavors?"

Tilting her head to allow him better access, she smiled. "Yes, I was out the better part of the day, and I found a whole new ensemble for tonight's *mysterious* activities. You know," she feigned a pout toward the mirror before continuing, "it'd be easier to shop, if you'd tell me more about our plans."

"All in due time, my dear, all in due time." He kissed her cheek, walked toward the dressing room, and called, "I can't wait to see tonight's ensemble."

When Tony reentered the bedroom on the way to his shower, he caught Claire's fiery gaze in the mirror. He'd learned to read her moods, and the fire he saw in the reflection wasn't a battle of wills—what he saw was desire. The way her cheeks reddened when their eyes met told him that she knew that she'd been caught. She'd been watching him with the expression of a girl looking through the candy store window. Totally nude, he moved behind her, wrapped her in his arms, and maneuvered his large hands beneath her flimsy robe. As he caressed her soft skin, he brushed his lips against her neck and whispered, "Do you think joining me in the shower would be detrimental to your hair and makeup?"

Goose bumps materialized on her arms and legs, as she breathlessly replied, "I think it would."

"Then perhaps we should plan it for another time?" His hands contradicted his words as they continued their descent.

"Or," Claire closed her eyes and tilted her head against his bare chest, "we could postpone your plans?"

Tony's body was obviously up for that idea, and the way she molded against him had his thoughts jumbled, but his mind prevailed. "Oh, God, I want to, but we have plenty of time for that. Tonight, I have special plans for you." He slowly stepped back, but before he relinquished his touch, he said, "And, so far, you look amazing. I believe I like your outfit now better than the one you bought."

With her robe now lying on the floor in a black silk puddle, Claire's cheeks blushed, and she flashed a modest smile. "It's November. I believe I'd get cold as we walk the streets of New York."

"Perhaps, but if I have anything to do with it—cold is *not* what you'd be feeling."

After a lingering kiss, Tony disappeared into the bathroom. He turned on the shower and with a groan, moved the levers to cold. When he emerged freshly showered and shaven, Claire looked amazing! After a little investigation, he learned that she was wearing some kind of hosiery that only went to her thigh. It was ingenious! Each step of obedience, each time she had the opportunity to disobey and didn't, his hope and anticipation for her answer was fortified.

After they'd eaten dinner and seen a play, Eric drove Tony and Claire to Central Park. The night was much cooler than Tony had planned; however, he was prepared for a carriage ride with gloves, scarves, and blankets. The longer the carriage moved, the happier Tony was for the cooler temperatures. It was as if no one else was out, and Central Park was lit up just for them.

He leaned close and began talking. It was something he'd never done to excess, until Claire—well, until her accident. Those days and weeks of talking just to talk had opened something inside of him. He had no desire to talk that much around others, but with Claire, he could. So, he did. As the horse trotted along the deserted paths, he talked about dating other women and how Claire was different. He explained that she knew the real him—the man few people ever get to see. Tony wanted her to understand, he had feelings—more than he'd ever experienced with anyone in his life. For the sake of the conversation and the proposal, he'd call them *love*. It wasn't that he thought his wording was deceitful. It was that he'd never experienced this feeling before, and he wasn't completely sure what it was—but, he believed it could be love.

"Claire, the other night you asked me if I cared about you. Honestly—with our initial arrangement—I never intended to, but without a doubt, I do." Tony looked down and took a deep breath. Resuming their eye contact, he asked, "Do you care about me? Do you enjoy being with me?"

He loved her smile and the way she never took her eyes off of him. "Tony, I do care about you. I want you to be happy, and I would do anything to help that happen, and on a night like tonight, or even a quiet night at home, I enjoy being with you," her eyes glistened in the cold air with the twinkling reflection of the lights from the trees, "more than enjoy; however," her eyes fluttered, "honestly, there are times I don't. There are times I want you away from me, or vice versa." Although her honesty may have been difficult to voice, she did just as he'd taught her and never looked away.

Tony smiled and leaned closer. He needed to kiss her. All he could think about was the taste of her lips. When he pulled away, he held nothing back, wanting her to know that not only did he expect honesty, he craved it. There were too many people in his life who were *yes men,* yet this woman who'd seen the absolute worst in him, could look him in the eye and be totally honest. "You're the most amazing woman. I have vice presidents, presidents, and chairmen of boards who've never experienced me as you have. None of them would have the courage to answer that question as honestly as you just did. It's your strength and determination that have infuriated me. That strength and resilience have also made me fall in love with you. Claire, I experienced life without you—after your accident."

He'd made his decision. Dr. Leonard wasn't the ultimate test: this was. She could walk away—he'd try to allow it. He would try, if that's what she wanted, but he had to know. He had to present the option.

He continued, "I don't want to be without you again, but I want you to make your own decision. Tonight, I'd like to present you with two options: your freedom—you may leave tonight and your debt is paid, or," he removed the ring he'd bought from his jacket pocket, "you could agree to marry me and spend the rest of your life with me, not out of obligation or contractual agreement, but because you want to be with me."

Perhaps Claire would think that his shaking was due to the cold. He waited. When she didn't reply, he said, "You told me yesterday no more black boxes, so I took it out of its box." He grinned. "Could we see if it fits?"

Claire nodded and extended her left hand, covered by a large mitten.

Tony smiled as he removed the fuzzy mitten and placed the ring on her fourth finger. "It seems to fit." Tony looked into her emerald eyes. "The question still seems to be unanswered. Do you want to keep it on and stay with me? Will you please be Claire Rawlings?"

"I-I'm so surprised," she stuttered, "ar-are you seriously asking *me* to marry *you*?"

He grinned and bowed his nose to hers. "Yes, my dear. This entire night has been leading to this proposal. I've watched you with me in private, in public, and with my closest friends. I want you there always. I love you."

"Please," she implored, "please, let me think. I promise you an answer soon."

He did what she asked. It wasn't often that Claire asked anything of him, and now she wanted time to think. As the carriage moved slowly around the frost-dusted park, Tony wondered how much time she wanted. Each moment made him more anxious. Maybe he hadn't thought this through enough. *What if she chose freedom? Could he do what he'd said? Could he give it to her?* As the panic continued to build a defensive wall, her beautiful voice broke through—shattering his doubts and calming his anxiety.

"God help me, yes—Tony, I'll marry you." He wrapped his arms around her and kissed her tenderly. When their lips separated, Claire confessed, "I love you too."

Relief like he'd never known filled his chest. Despite the frigid temperatures, he was warm and satisfied. Her confession of love was the most wonderful thing he'd ever heard.

The next morning, Tony slipped from their bed and made his way down to his office. He didn't care that it was Thanksgiving morning. He had a wedding to plan, and he wanted it done—now. Glancing at the clock, 7:03 AM, he knew who he needed to call first.

He'd discussed his plans with Catherine, and since Claire's conversation with Dr. Leonard, Catherine's opinion of Claire, too, had softened. She even told Tony more than once that she thought Claire was *good for him.* Funny, that was also what Courtney had said. It was more than that. Catherine spent hours and hours working with Claire and helping her recover from her accident. Tony suspected that it reminded Catherine of her own accident years ago. She knew firsthand the difficult path Claire endured, both mentally and physically. She understood it in a way Tony never would. That common experience created a bond between the two women. Of course, Catherine never admitted that, but she did say that when Tony was with Claire, especially during her recovery, Catherine saw Nathaniel in him. Although, Tony hadn't witnessed Nathaniel and Marie's interaction during that time, he knew a compliment when he heard one.

Despite all of that, Tony wasn't sure how Catherine honestly felt about the marriage thing. He squared his shoulders and hit *CALL.* Catherine answered on the second ring. "Yes?"

"Good morning, Marie."

"Anton... you have heard of holidays, haven't you?"

"I thought you would want to be the first to hear my news—*our* news."

Catherine gasped. "You did it, didn't you? You asked her and she said yes?"

"Yes, and she's very anxious for your reaction."

"You actually *asked* her?" She emphasized the word.

"Yes—I *asked* her."

"And she said yes?"

Tony grinned into his phone. "Should I be offended that you find this so difficult to believe?"

"No, you shouldn't. I'm just—just—pleased. I think you're right. The situation couldn't go on the way it was much longer. This makes perfect sense. Besides, I can tell... it's what you want."

"I do," Tony agreed.

"Did you offer her an alternative?"

"Her freedom."

"Oh, Anton, what if she'd gone that way?"

"She didn't."

Catherine's tone hardened. "Tell me how this changes things."

"It doesn't. Like you just said, it's a continuation."

"She'll have your name. Things will change."

Although his office door was closed, Tony lowered his voice. "She'll share the name *Rawlings*. You know as well as I, that she'll never be able to share *my* name and we both know why."

"Do you? Do you remember? It's important that you remember."

"Marie, how could I forget? I remember as well as you."

"Are you *in love* with her?"

Tony hesitated. "I believe I am."

"And you don't believe that changes anything."

"Maybe it does," Tony conceded. "Maybe it changes her role, but it doesn't change her debt. Now it has become a debt that she'll pay forever. That's the way this works, right? *Forever*—until death do us part?"

"No, Anton, it goes beyond that. I can promise you that."

He sat taller. "It may not have been the original plan, but once she says *I do*, there'll be one less Nichols."

"You believe that, don't you?"

"Don't you?" Tony asked. "Tell me that we haven't changed her and made her into a Rawlings."

"She has changed. I see that." Catherine conceded.

"I've helped you and you've helped me. Can I continue to count on your assistance?"

Catherine's tone softened. "Yes, of course, Anton. Nathaniel intended for us to work together. I won't be the one to disappoint him."

"I'm glad to hear that. Neither will I."

In a professional tone, Catherine replied, "Mr. Rawlings, please tell the future Mrs. Rawlings that I'm very happy for both of you."

Tony smiled. "I'll do that. Marie?"

"Yes?"

"This has worked out much better than I ever imagined, and I know it wouldn't have without you."

"Anton, I agree with everything, but please don't forget the big picture."

"I've told you that I'm in control, and we've seen that over and over—with Dr. Leonard and with my proposal. Now the whole world will know that she belongs to me—it won't be a clandestine arrangement."

"The whole world?" Catherine asked. "Is that referring to the emails you've been receiving from Emily Vandersol?"

Tony grinned. "As a matter of fact—yes. The Vandersols will be joining us for Thanksgiving dinner. Soon, they'll learn that Claire belongs to me. Her interaction with them will be at my discretion."

"Oh!" Catherine exclaimed. "How I wish I were a fly on the wall."

"My dear Marie, technology is a wonderful thing. Help yourself."

"Thank you, Mr. Rawlings, I believe I will. I'll also show the future Mrs. Rawlings my extreme pleasure upon your return."

Tony smirked. "That'll be interesting to witness. We'll be returning on Saturday. I'll let you know when I know more about the wedding."

"You know me—always at your service," she quipped.

Tony grinned as he hit *DISCONNECT*.

After some coffee and a light breakfast, Tony made the rest of his calls, and within a few hours, he had the whole wedding thing underway. The next hurdle was quickly approaching. Within a matter of hours he'd have the opportunity to meet his future in-laws face-to-face. They weren't exactly strangers. He knew everything about them and had even been at their wedding. Tony smirked; now, they'd be coming to his. Sometimes he marveled at how strangely things come full circle. That wasn't really true. He'd know that they were at his wedding; they'd had no idea.

With a few hours before his surprise guests arrived, Tony decided to go upstairs. He wanted to visit his fiancée, tell her about their wedding plans, and enjoy what was his for the taking. Besides, with their impending visitors, it was never too early to remind the future Mrs. Rawlings that her change of name would not mean a change in his rules.

Chapter 10

Just another symposium—September 2011

(Consequences—Chapter 42)

———◆———

Everyone has to make their own decisions. You just have to be able to accept the consequences without complaining.
—Grace Jones

RISK VERSUS FAILURE IN THE WORLD OF BUSINESS—that was the title they'd given him. Tony wondered sometimes how they came up with this crap! Three years ago the bottom fell out of the damn economy and he'd survived. It seemed as though some of these symposiums and seminars were trying to tell the up-and-coming entrepreneurs that the failure was the fault of business. That wasn't entirely true, but voicing his true feelings wouldn't win him any supporters in the necessary arenas. So, every now and then, he'd concede to play their game and talk their talk.

Inspirational—that was what the planners called him, as they crooned, gushed, and requested his presence at their seminar. Shelly received invitations like this all of the time. More often than not, she turned them down. After all, Tony was a busy man; however, every now and then, she'd ask him to consider attending. She'd remind him that he needed to do the occasional public-relations outreach. It not only kept his name on the tips of people's tongues, sometimes he found talent along the way.

As he delivered the keynote address, Tony talked about recognizing and weighing risks. He discussed the importance of knowing your opponents and competitors, as well as your customers and investors—he admonished the audience to be informed. Don't be blindsided—be prepared. The people in the crowd hung on his every word. After all, he was Anthony Rawlings.

The act of delivering the occasional speech wasn't new; he'd been doing it forever. The newness came in that he didn't mind doing it as much as he once had. Looking to his left and seeing the emerald gaze, his business smile morphed into a genuine grin. The way Mrs. Rawlings watched and listened to his every word fulfilled an emptiness that he never knew existed. Many of the magazines and tabloids referred to Claire as nothing more than an ornament to adorn Tony's arm. That wasn't true. She was so much more.

Without a doubt, she was much smarter than the press gave her credit. It wasn't just her education—she was also a quick learner; however, when it came to her degree, Tony was thankful that Claire never mentioned pursuing meteorology. Other than a night a long, long time ago, in a bar, in a faraway land, the subject never came up. As a rule, Tony enjoyed fulfilling Claire's requests. He liked the entire process. He liked being asked and watching her techniques of persuasion. Most of the time, he enjoyed granting her desires; however, if she'd asked to return to the world of weather, he'd have denied it, without thinking twice. Since last December, Claire's full-time job was him. She was his wife—Mrs. Anthony Rawlings—and as such had no time for other endeavors. When he allowed her to enter the spotlight as his fiancée and wife, Tony hadn't realized the many roles she'd be required to perform. He didn't manufacture the responsibilities—they just were. With each new task, Claire succeeded. Whether it was charity work, hosting a party, or being at his side, he was constantly awed by her perfection. Perhaps he shouldn't have been. After all, as a Rawlings, nothing less would be acceptable. Public failure could not be tolerated. She handled her responsibilities well.

On occasions such as this particular seminar, after the speeches were complete, Tony was expected to mingle with the attendees. Claire was the one with that talent. She possessed an uncanny ability to talk to anyone and was the master of small talk. With a smile on her face, she could move people through the process, keep him from being saddled with one person too long, and most importantly, get them out.

Once his speech was done and he sat, Claire's small hand moved to his thigh. No one could see below the table, yet her light touch combined with her beautiful smile gave him a sense of accomplishment as he'd never known. A grin, a touch, and suddenly the evening was not only tolerable, but enjoyable.

Every now and then while the speeches continued, she'd whisper something to him—most of the time it had nothing to do with what was being said. It might be an observation of someone in the audience, or something totally random. It was strange how that, too, could make him relax. Externally, he was calm, cool, and professional, just as he'd always been. Tony recognized the difference—it was internal.

Sometimes he'd think back to a year and a half ago in sheer wonderment. The woman next to him was so different than the woman he met in Atlanta. Claire had exceeded his expectations at every test and turn. Tony knew that the same could be said of Catherine's expectations. Eighteen months ago, Catherine begrudgingly agreed to assist in overseeing Claire's care. Today, she was Claire's biggest cheerleader. As such, she'd articulate accolades at Claire's success with each new test or challenge. Catherine would remind Tony how proud Nathaniel would be of what he'd accomplished. He successfully removed a Nichols—a child of a child—while keeping her in a blissfully unaware state of debt.

With the attendees waning, Mr. and Mrs. Anthony Rawlings stood, still surrounded by a handful of eager entrepreneurs. Claire seemed to know that Tony's personal time clock was about to expire and graciously moved each man or woman on as soon as possible. There were still a few people waiting for their chance to speak with him when a blonde-headed young man approached. "Hello, Mr. Rawlings, I'm pleased to meet you. Your speech was remarkable and inspiring." Tony shook his hand and politely thanked him, and then the young man continued, "I have an unusual request. May I speak with your wife for a few minutes?"

Tony's glare immediately went to his wife. Moments earlier she'd been the perfect companion, yet in a split second, he saw her well-polished mask shatter into a thousand pieces. There was something in her eyes, a look, a feeling, one he'd seen in pictures, and then it was gone.

It all happened so fast. Then, she seemed to remember her place and worked to recover. She placed her hand gently on Tony's arm and stuttered, "O-Oh my," "A-Anthony," "S-Simon." She swallowed. "Anthony, may I introduce Simon Johnson. Simon and I were students together at Valparaiso—a million years ago." Each word came faster than the last. "Simon, may I introduce my husband, Anthony Rawlings."

The two men locked eyes and shook hands again. Tony hadn't seen Simon Johnson in years. He'd actually spoken to him a few times in California. Although he remembered the man was truly gifted in the world of gaming, that wasn't forefront in Tony's mind. He remembered pictures from the private investigators—pictures of two young people, practically children, head over heels in love. Suddenly, Tony's world came to a screeching halt. *Was the love he'd seen in those pictures ever anything he'd seen in the woman who professed her love for him?* Even her smiles today were different. *Was it age and maturity, or did this man possess a piece of Anthony's wife's heart that Tony would never have?* Summoning his most affirmable voice, Tony replied, "I believe that's Mrs. Rawlings' decision."

It didn't take Claire long to choose Simon over Tony. She willingly, without regret, excused the two of them and left him standing all alone. Before he brought Claire to these events, Tony would usually bring Patricia. He didn't enjoy her company nearly as well; however, Tony was sure she'd never have left him hanging in the middle of a room of people all alone.

Anthony Rawlings continued to smile and shake hands. He listened to questions and proposals and said all the right things; however, his eyes and mind were constantly pulled to a table not terribly far away. To Claire's credit, when Simon attempted physical contact, Tony watched her pull away. For what seemed like hours the two of them appeared engaged in a soul-searching discussion. When Claire finally returned, he scrutinized her expression. It was perfect and empty. He never realized that he'd been denied that *look*, until he saw it bestowed on someone else. Stoically he nodded and addressed his wife, "Mrs. Rawlings." They had more attendees to meet, and her name was his subtle reminder of her title and her duty. *She belonged to him!*

Tony glanced at his watch. Claire had only been gone for eight minutes. It was the longest eight minutes he'd endured in a lifetime. The rest of the evening, she performed beyond expectation. She spoke politely and moved people along. It was her eyes: they were far away in another time and another place.

As they stepped to the curb and waited for Eric, Tony's hand rested in the small of Claire's back. He, too, was seeing memories— flashes of photos. He remembered pictures of Claire and Simon on the

Valparaiso campus and reports of her staying in Simon's room, or vice-versa.

When they were settled into the limousine, Tony waited. He waited for Claire to talk, to apologize, or to say anything. She didn't. Her normally chatty demeanor was gone; instead she stared aimlessly toward the window, seemingly mesmerized by the lights of Chicago. Time didn't register as Tony's blood boiled. *How dare Simon Johnson approach Anthony Rawlings' wife in a public setting? Claire knew her role; it was that of the perfect companion. How many rules had she successfully broken in a matter of seconds? By leaving him and going off with Simon, she'd not fulfilled her obligation, in essence, not doing as she'd been told. She did it in public! It was public failure!* Tony wondered how many tabloids would jump on this.

Finally, he spoke, "Mrs. Rawlings." He moved closer. Their noses nearly touched when she turned to face him. "What is your name?"

It was as if his words weren't registering. He wanted—no *needed* for her to understand. Tony grasped her chin, not allowing her to turn away, and repeated his question. "Your name. What is your name?"

He watched as the fire in her eyes began to burn away the fog of memories. "Tony, what are you doing?"

He held tight. "I'm asking you a question. One that you seem unable to answer."

Claire's neck stiffened. "My name is Claire... Claire Rawlings."

"Please, Mrs. Rawlings, explain to me how you can be sitting with me, your husband, wearing the rings I purchased, in the limousine paid for by my hard work, and thinking about another man."

"Tony, please let go of my face. You're hurting me."

Though the red seeped, he remembered his promise and released her chin; however, relinquishing her completely was out of the question. His large hand slid behind her neck, tightly holding her head, and purposely pulling the hair that dangled down her neck. Tony did not like repeating himself, and he'd already done it once since they entered the limousine. For Claire's sake, he didn't want to do it again. He continued, "Do I need to repeat every question, or do you think you may be able to answer at least one the first time?"

"Seeing Simon caught me off guard. I haven't thought of or heard from him in eight years. Don't you think that deserves some reflection?"

She gasped as his grip tightened. "No," he growled. "I believe the past is just that. It's done and now it's time to concentrate on the present." He stared at the fire that now burnt out of control as the car's cabin filled with his pent-up rage. *How dare she be thinking about another man!* He spoke slowly and deliberately, wanting to give her the chance to hear every word. Anthony Rawlings would not repeat himself again. "At present, I believe you need to concentrate on showing me that *my* wife is first and foremost concerned with pleasing her husband."

With their eyes still locked, Tony reached for the button to close the window between them and Eric. Claire didn't look away until she noticed his next move. With the hand not holding his wife's neck, Tony unzipped the slacks of his tuxedo. He wasn't truly thinking—he was reacting. That didn't matter. When Claire began to protest, he trumped her. Physically she was no match for him, and the idea that she'd attempt to push herself away may have been comical if it hadn't fueled his rage. Tony seized her hand and twisted it back. Holding her neck, he rested his head against the leather seat, entwined his fingers in her hair and directed her movement. It didn't take her long to remember how to follow his number-one rule. Not all demands required audible words. He'd trained her well.

Before they left the limousine, Tony told Claire to fix her makeup; there would be people in the building where they were about to enter. The world didn't need to know that his wife needed a refresher course on appropriate behavior. Dutifully, Claire appeared composed as they walked through Trump Tower's lobby, yet when he gently put his arm around her waist, she tensed. It was enough insubordination to tell Tony that Claire's lessons were not complete. He leaned close and whispered, "I have more ways you can demonstrate your devotion, Mrs. Rawlings. We'll review when we reach our apartment."

———◆◆◆———

TONY WOKE DURING the night. They'd be heading to Iowa in the morning, yet his head pounded with the memories of Simon Johnson. Once they were back to the apartment, Claire had done her best to show her devotion. Tony reminded himself that she wouldn't have misbehaved if Simon had not approached her. That didn't absolve her of her inappropriate behavior. He planned to remind her about her duties, again, once they returned to the estate. A breach like what occurred couldn't be repeated. Perhaps she needed some time alone at the estate, showing her devotion to her husband, instead of out with friends or communicating with her sister. Perhaps that would help to reinforce his stance. After all, he couldn't tolerate public failure.

Claire's consequences weren't enough to quell Tony's fury. Simon Johnson was also guilty. He'd had the audacity to approach Tony's wife in a public forum. Tony slipped from their bed and made his way to his apartment office where he pulled out his private laptop.

He began to search Simon Johnson. The man had made quite a success of himself. He was founder of a gaming company in Palo Alto, California, called SiJo Gaming. Though not as wealthy as Tony, he was doing very well. It seemed as though he'd left Shedis-tics, a Rawlings subsidiary, years before. If he still worked under the Rawlings umbrella, Tony thought he could influence Johnson through business. After all, Tony had done it before; however, this was different.

Johnson's success made him a potential threat. Tony wanted Claire totally dependent upon him. He couldn't allow there to be an ex-boyfriend with the financial means to help Claire if she asked. By the way Johnson looked at her, and she at him, that wasn't beyond the realm of possibility.

If business intervention weren't possible, Tony needed to look elsewhere. In an unnamed file, he found the cell phone number he sought.

The way he looked at it, it was a business decision. Claire's behavior reflected upon him; he had a reputation to uphold. He'd invested a lot of time and money into his wife. As with anything else in business, he evaluated the facts. Positives were accentuated and negatives needed to be eliminated. If an adversary was identified, it became a liability. Liabilities can hinder the projected outcome—and needed to be removed.

Admittedly, this was different than any other call he'd authorized. Simon Johnson was not on Nathaniel's list. That didn't mean that Tony couldn't justify his decision.

Claire was on his list, and as long as she performed well and personified a Rawlings, Tony was doing his part to rid the world of a Nichols—a child of a child. When she failed, when she exhibited her independence and innate strength in a non-Rawlings matter, she reminded Tony that he'd failed to directly, fully fulfill Nathaniel's directive. In order to avoid this type of a failure in the future, ridding the world of Simon Johnson would work to assure Claire's success. He was helping her.

After the short call, Tony made his way back to their bed. He felt a slight twinge of his conscience when he found Claire sleeping on her edge of the massive mattress. It was how she used to sleep when he first brought her to the estate. He wanted to pull her close and apologize for some of his earlier behavior, but that wouldn't teach her the lesson he needed her to learn. It would only show weakness, and that wasn't acceptable.

When they returned to the estate, Claire's disobedience would result in new rules, and her recently earned liberties would need to be reevaluated. It only made sense: actions had consequences. Nevertheless, by the time he slid under the covers, the sound of Claire's soft breathing and the knowledge of his call dissipated the last hues of red. With a renewed sense of calm, Tony drifted off to sleep.

Chapter 11

The beginning of the end ... coffee?
—January 2012

(Consequences—Chapter 46)

If a relationship is to evolve,
it must go through a series of endings.
—Lisa Moriyama

TONY PACED THE length of his office. Although his decision was set, he couldn't shake the conflicted feeling that nagged deep inside of him. He told himself that this was a test—only a test. He'd presented Claire with more tests than he could count, and when she passed this one, everything could continue as it had been. *Would she pass?* Tony knew in his heart that this wasn't the same as other tests he'd created; this was bigger and potentially life changing. It wasn't a *test:* it was her *final examination*—the fulfillment of a personal deal he'd made a lifetime ago. It started out as an idea, a seed, and like things do, it grew.

Twenty-two months ago, when he brought Claire to his home, Tony didn't know what to expect. He never in a million years planned to have feelings for her—she was the enemy, a Nichols. In hindsight,

Catherine had seen and warned him. She knew his interest in Claire was more than that of curiosity. That being said, Tony fought those feelings with all he had. He'd never admit it to anyone, but in a significant way, Claire was his biggest success and his biggest failure. He'd brought her to Iowa to pay the penance of her family's sins, but during her sentence she'd won him over. Oh, he'd changed her, but she'd changed him, too. He was no longer her warden but her husband. In essence, she'd derailed his plans.

Unlike any other failure, and he'd had very few, Tony didn't mind. He enjoyed her—more than enjoyed, he craved her. She fulfilled a part of him he'd never known existed, yet despite all the ways he'd changed her, he knew that she was still a Nichols. She acted, dressed, and looked different, but was it real? After all, deep down, she was still the same woman who he'd acquired. It was a reality he couldn't shake. Maybe it was the way the subject snuck into conversations. Catherine would say something like, *I saw the photos of the two of you in the magazine. Claire is doing so well, and you two truly make a handsome couple. Sometimes I forget that she's a Nichols.*

It would be at times like that when Tony would remember the little seed that had been planted decades ago—the seed which grew tall and deep and reminded him that a *Nichols* helped to condemn his grandfather to twenty-two months in prison. That time period resonated in Tony's psyche. *Twenty-two months*—the length of time that Nathaniel Rawls lost to the state of New York for sins that were saddled on him by Sherman Nichols and Jonathon Burke. With that time period in mind, Claire's sentence was almost up. Originally, it had been the time period Tony had hoped to keep Claire. He and Catherine had even discussed what would happen to her once it was all over.

Since the very beginning, Catherine had reminded him that Tony needed to stay cognizant of his public persona. If Claire failed, Tony needed to be prepared to distance himself. If he couldn't, there was only one option. That option may have been viable two years ago, but it wasn't something Tony would entertain now. Claire's *accident* had been too traumatic. He refused to consider her enduring anything worse; nevertheless, the groundwork had been laid for the option of public disgrace.

From Tony's perspective, the decision was hers. The only way that Claire would be publicly disgraced was if she failed the test he was about to present. If she passed, the time period of her sentence would pass and life would go on. Taking a stiff drink of Johnnie Walker Scotch, Tony reassured himself that Claire would pass. She'd been presented with the option of freedom once, the night he proposed, and she willingly surrendered her liberties to him. Standing near the highboy, Tony poured himself another two fingers—maybe three—of scotch when he heard his office door open.

"Anton, it's late. Why are you still up?"

He didn't turn around; instead, he glanced at his watch—2:14 AM. He had no idea it was that late. "I'm thinking."

"Where's Claire?" Catherine asked.

"Bed." He spun around. "Where would you expect her to be at this hour?"

"She's in *your* suite, isn't she? You left her alone in there?"

"What's the matter, Catherine? No videos for you tonight?"

Catherine shook her head and sat on the leather sofa. "Anton, you're upset. Are you worried?"

He lifted one finger in her direction and went to his desk. After a few moments and a few codes, he stood and faced his oldest colleague. "No, I'm not worried. I have total confidence in my wife. Tomorrow night you and I'll be discussing how she followed my rules, once again."

"I believe you're right. So, why are you doing this?" Her shoulders sagged. "Why are you forcing her to jump through another hoop?" With more determination, she stood and faced him. "Claire loves you and you love her. Let that be enough. There are other Nichols who can pay. Look what you've done to John." Her eyes glistened. "Oh, Anton, that was brilliant."

Tony exhaled and collapsed on the chair near the sofa. "That had its own perks, but it was also a step of this test. Don't you understand? Now John can't help her—so much for his proclamation of undying devotion. He and Emily are a little busy at the moment."

"I do! I understand, and the Simmonses? They're still out of the country. Right?"

He studied Catherine's expression. "Right. Why would that matter? They're *my* friends. Brent works for me."

"Oh, you're right. It's just that I believe Claire and Mrs. Simmons have become very close."

Tony shrugged. "I don't know. Claire complains about how much Courtney talks." A small grin emerged. "Now, if that's not the pot—"

"Anton, I see how you have this all planned. Nathaniel would be so proud. And you're so brave! You're willing to take the poison?"

His dark eyes darted from his near empty glass to Catherine's questioning gaze. "I am. I don't think it'll be necessary, but if she takes the bait and drives away, I'll drink it." He swallowed the remaining contents of his tumbler. "Are you sure you know what you're doing?"

Catherine nodded. "It's not like I can practice on anyone, but yes. I'm confident you'll go unconscious and nothing more."

"As in, I won't die? Go ahead and say it, Marie. I've momentarily turned off the surveillance to the whole damn house. The whole system's doing a reboot. No one will ever hear what we're saying."

"Anton, I don't want to talk about you dying—that's not going to happen. As you've said, you probably won't even need to drink the coffee. But, if you do—"

"If I do, I'll live to see the repercussions of Claire's decision."

Catherine nodded. "What about witnesses?"

"I have a web conference I'm doing from home tomorrow. If she gets in the car, I'll be live in front of people all over the country."

Catherine reached out and covered Tony's hand. "If you're sure you need to do this, I'll help you. Just like I've helped in the past and how you've helped me. I won't let anything happen to you. We're too close to seeing the fulfillment of our goals." She clapped her hands under her chin. "Just think—the end is so near. Only Emily will be left."

Tony straightened his shoulders and sat taller. "Remember that— only Emily. Claire will be done. Nothing else is necessary; her name is off the list."

"Yes, of course. That's what you'd said, but if she doesn't take the bait?"

His voice deepened. "Then her name is off the list. If she's presented with a clear line to freedom and doesn't take it. No! *When* she's presented with this avenue and doesn't take it, it'll prove that Claire Nichols is gone." He felt his eyes darken as he emphasized his final point, spacing each word. "Claire. Rawlings. Was. Never. On. Our. List."

Catherine stood. "Yes, of course. Now, how much longer until the cameras turn back on? I'll get things set in the kitchen."

Tony glanced at his watch. "You have about ten minutes."

Walking toward the door, she said, "I'll have it ready."

Looking into his empty tumbler, Tony's mind filled with images of him and his wife. They were memories of private times, times of comfort and companionship. He'd never had a person in his life before. He'd never wanted to be near someone or please someone. He had to know that, no matter what, he could trust this person. *Why, oh why had that person been Claire?* Of all of the people in the world, why did it have to be one of the people he'd promised to bring down?

Closing his eyes, Tony remembered Claire after her accident. He had brought her down, but in true Claire fashion, she rebounded. That strength and resilience amazed him. *If she failed this impending examination, would she rebound?*

He didn't want to think about it; instead, he imagined their future. Claire would pass. She wouldn't take the bait.

Feeling a bit more confident, Tony walked back to his desk and searched travel sites. Claire enjoyed travel. She didn't know that she was facing a life-changing test, but when she passed, he wanted to reward her. Maybe England? They'd talked about that. No, it was January. The United Kingdom would be cold. A grin surfaced as he thought about her likes and dislikes—she liked sun. He entered *tropical beaches* into the search engine. Tony would take her someplace warm. If she asked why, he'd say it was because she was upset about her brother-in-law; however, he'd know the real reason: it was her positive consequence.

When Tony crawled back into his bed, he slid behind Claire's sleeping body and wrapped her in his arms. She fit perfectly as he was drawn to her radiating warmth. Gently kissing her hair, he tasted her perfume as his hands wandered her curves, caressing her soft skin. Her soft murmurs filled his heart with hope as she settled into his embrace. Smiling, Tony imagined that in a few days he'd have his wife on a sunny beach with nothing more than a bikini—maybe not even that. Those images and more filled his mind as he drifted off to sleep.

When he woke, Tony lingered longer than usual in the warmth of their bed. Being much too early for Claire to wake, he lifted his head, rested it on his elbow, and watched her sleep. Her lightened hair covered her pillow as renegade strands crisscrossed her cheek. Along with her exposed face, one bare shoulder was visible above the mound of luxurious blankets. Tony leaned closer, kissed her forehead, and watched in amusement as her nose wrinkled. Lightly, he kissed her again. This time he was rewarded with the most beautiful moan as she stretched and turned toward him. Although Claire was still sound asleep, she subconsciously responded to his touch. He wanted to wake her, but he feared that if her warm, soft skin touched his and they connected their bodies, as they'd been connected the night before, he wouldn't be able to carry out his plan.

Brushing the strands of blonde from her face, he whispered, "You don't need to wake yet." When she didn't respond and he was confident of her sleeping, he added, "You have a big day, my dear. You need your rest. Tonight we'll celebrate."

Throughout Tony's morning routine, he avoided thoughts of Claire's impending examination. To him it was merely a formality—the final signature on their life-long contract. The deal was already complete; she belonged to him. His wife wouldn't disappoint.

Anthony Rawlings reassured himself. Claire knew better than to disappoint, because if she did, he'd promised consequences, and above everything else, he was a man of his word.

Tony had finished his breakfast when Claire entered the dining room. She'd obviously just gotten out of bed and in his opinion was the most beautiful woman in the world. It was part of her appeal, a piece of the puzzle that helped Tony realize that he had truly fallen in love. She didn't have to be wearing designer dresses nor have her hair and makeup perfect. Even without the polish, she was stunning. Smiling he said, "Good morning, my dear. You look beautiful this morning."

Claire made a face. "I think you need an eye exam." She wrapped her arms around his neck, and he stared up into the emerald glow of her eyes. Before he could speak, she kissed his cheek and continued, "I just wanted to catch you before you left."

It was then that Tony's attention went to Catherine. She'd silently entered the dining room, and at Claire's comment about Tony's departure, Catherine's lips pursed into a straight line. As Claire sat and Catherine poured her coffee, Claire continued speaking. "I wanted to tell you how much I appreciated talking to Emily. It's a difficult time for them, and I wanted to let you know I'll miss you."

It wasn't just her words that reassured Tony: it was her smile. She knew her contact with her family was at his discretion, and she wasn't fighting, but thanking him for it. He was glad Catherine heard. The crimson that had been threatening faded. Tony proceeded with confidence. "Good news, I'm working from home today." He settled back against the chair as Catherine slipped wordlessly from the room. "So, you won't need to miss me."

"That's great!" Claire replied. "Do you have a lot of work?"

"A few web conferences and phone calls, but don't worry, I know your schedule is free. I have some ideas for us, too." Tony knew that his smile was too big for the circumstances; nevertheless, he couldn't restrain it. Claire would pass her test, and he had multiple ideas for celebration in mind. He couldn't wait to tell her about the surprise trip. He'd found it earlier this morning when he was supposed to be preparing for his web conference. It was a small exclusive resort on Seven Mile Beach on the west side of Grand Cayman Island. Currently, the temperatures were in the mid to upper eighties and the forecast was perfect. He imagined her delight as he showed her the website.

Claire replied, "All right, I need to work out and clean up. I came down here in a hurry to see you."

"When you're dressed, come to my office," he said. As he stood to leave, he reached out. Mindlessly, he touched her shoulder and fought the urge to explore below her soft robe. His desire to speed time and move past the examination was almost palpable.

She tilted her head toward his hand and said, "I'll be there as soon as I can."

Kissing her cheek, he allowed his desire to infiltrate his tone. "Or, you could visit before you dress?"

She touched his hand. "If I do that, you may not get your work done."

Damn, she was right. They would have plenty of time for his plans. "As usual, my dear, you're right. I'll see you in my office, soon." As his lips brushed her cheek, he looked up in time to see gray irises watching from the hall. Reluctantly, he left his wife and walked toward his office.

Before he closed the door, Catherine hurriedly came down the hall. Everything they said at this point would be on video. They both knew what could be at stake. "Mr. Rawlings, you left the dining room before I could check on you. Is there anything you need?"

"No, Catherine, I believe I'm quite satisfied with all that I have."

She squared her shoulders. "You are planning on working from home?" Her tone made the statement a question. "Or have your plans changed?"

"Nothing has changed. I'll let you know if I need anything."

Catherine nodded and turned away.

After a brief visit to the Grand Cayman's website, Tony forced himself to concentrate on the business at hand. He had a web conference with some other investors about a joint endeavor that hadn't yielded the desired results. It was a bold initiative to revitalize manufacturing in Michigan. In desperate need of help, the auto companies and the state had been more than willing to make concessions regarding taxes and fees. The problem centered on the expiration of the original terms. It seemed as though the powers that be in the state of Michigan believed that they had Tony and the other investors over the proverbial barrel. As far as he was concerned, it couldn't be farther from the truth. Reviewing the numbers, Tony knew that he'd gladly take the write-off and shut the doors before he agreed to the exorbitant taxes. He'd already shut the doors of an unprofitable stamping plant in Flint, Michigan. He didn't understand how they could think he was bluffing on this.

It was almost 10:00 AM when Tony heard the faint knock on his office door. Despite his conversation at hand, a grin briefly flew across his lips as he read the time on his screen. His rules regarding Claire spending her days with him in his office no longer existed. She was, after all, his wife; however, it seemed that old habits die hard. When she'd first been told that she needed to spend the days he worked from home, nearby, in the event her services were required, he'd told her to *always* be present by 10:00 AM. Even though he didn't say that this morning, nor did he require her services, her obedience continued to strengthen his confidence. He pushed the button under his desk and his door opened. Before he could acknowledge her presence, he needed to respond to one of the other investors. Claire didn't interrupt; she smiled and sat quietly on the sofa. Later he noticed her reading an article in one of the magazines.

The conference finally finished around 10:45 AM. He'd tried to end it sooner, as he wanted to appreciate every second they had together before her test. She must have heard that his conference ended, because when he turned his chair, she was looking in his direction. Immediately, she placed the magazine on the table and walked toward him. Grinning, he murmured, "Ahh, blue, my favorite color." Tony was suddenly thankful for his loose-fitting sweatpants. "You're beautiful in any color." He drank her in, savoring everything about her. His eyes settled on her diamond journey necklace. He knew why Catherine had laid it out: it helped to create the persona that Claire enjoyed the finer things. Nevertheless, he'd always liked it. Lowering his gaze to the neckline of her sweater, his tone turned sultry. "Or, in no color." Putting his hands around her waist, Tony longed to pull Claire onto his lap and whisper, *follow my rules—I know you can.* If he did, would it ruin the test? He could say it loud and proud. Anthony Rawlings wasn't hiding from anyone; instead, he caressed her trim waist and said, "I have one more web conference at 11:00 AM and then two lunch phone calls. I'd like you back after that." It wasn't a request: it was a demand or a plea. He wasn't sure anymore.

"It's so nice out. I'd like to go for a hike while you're working."

"No." Tony slowed his tone. He couldn't give anything away. "The phone calls may need to be postponed, depending on the outcome of the next web conference. I'd like you here, if I'm done earlier. We can lunch and discuss our possible afternoon activities." He turned back to his computer screen and read while he spoke. It was the message he'd planted, the next step. As he was about to continue, Claire surprised him with kisses to his neck.

Warm breaths instigated chills, as Claire responded. "Well, then, may I just go out back? The sky's so clear, and I could really use some fresh air."

He didn't try to contain his seductive grin. "Okay, just be back by noon, and..." It was now or never. "...could you get me some coffee before you go?"

Each move she made filled him with hope and desire. His arousal was nicely hidden, but as soon as she left, he definitely needed to reposition his seating. One more kiss to his neck and Claire said, "Yes."

At 10:57 AM, Claire returned to his desk with a warm cup of coffee. When he heard her approaching, he picked up his iPhone and pretended to have a conversation as he rummaged through papers on his desk. When he *hung up*, he turned and faced his wife. Tony's body battled with his mind as he fought his personal desire. It was the confidence of her impending behavior that propelled him forward. "Tell Eric there are contracts at the Iowa City office. I need them here *before* 1:00 PM. He needs to get them immediately." For a moment, Claire stood silently and stared with her big, innocent emerald eyes. A small voice told him that she knew his plan, she was ahead of him and—and—he waited for the voice to tell him if she would pass. Then he remembered her earlier request. Claire didn't know his plans; she wanted to walk outside. Exhaling the building tension, he added, "And after that, you may go for your walk. Just be back by noon."

She smiled and kissed his cheek. "Okay. I'll tell Eric and be back." He watched as she hurried away. The web conference was to begin in two minutes, yet he felt as though his life was literally walking toward her destiny. He adjusted his computer screen and pulled up the house surveillance.

Sitting on the edge of his desk, where she'd placed it, was his coffee. Tony looked at the cup. He'd never asked Catherine the specifics about the contents. He had no reason to distrust her. She said he'd wake after he drank it. Tony knew that Catherine would not disappoint him.

The conference began as each participant introduced him or herself. Tony listened halfheartedly as he scanned their resumes. They were the pages he'd been ruffling through earlier. He heard their voices and put names with their faces; all the while he watched the small section of his screen devoted to the garages.

After he'd introduced himself and given a synopsis of the goals he planned to accomplish during the next thirty minutes, he watched Claire enter the garage. Briefly, she gazed at the cars and then walked toward Eric's apartment door. The small image didn't have sound, but he could see as she knocked and Eric opened his door. It seemed as though Eric answered a little too quickly; after all, he was expecting Claire, but Claire didn't seem to notice.

The exchange between her and Eric lasted only seconds, but as the cup of coffee taunted him, Tony felt as if time were standing still. Then the examination he'd prepared unfolded before his eyes. Eric grabbed his coat and hat, unlocked the key cabinet on the wall, removed a set of keys, and shut the cabinet. Tony held his breath as the small metal door bounced open. It wasn't overt and Eric didn't appear to notice. He was still speaking with Claire as he looked at his watch. Next, the garage door opened to the outside world as sunlight streamed over the camera, fading the color from the corner of Tony's screen.

On the larger image, two participants discussed something about a quantitative summary. Tony didn't care. His attention was on the small corner where Claire wrapped her arms around her midsection and watched Eric drive away. Color returned to the image as the garage door closed. She turned back to the way she'd entered when she stopped and stared toward the open cabinet.

Tony didn't know what was being said on his web conference as he held his breath and waited. Seconds earlier, time had stood still; now he couldn't slow it down. Claire reached into the cabinet and grabbed a set of keys. The ones to the new Mercedes were purposely placed in a more accessible spot. The headlights flashed as she hit the button on the fob.

When the garage door opened again, Tony didn't notice the loss of color. His vision, his office, his life was red. The disappointment was overwhelming. The pain of betrayal washed over him as the crimson-colored memories sped through his consciousness. Everything—all twenty-two months—was a lie. Claire never loved him. If she had, she wouldn't have jumped at the first opportunity to leave. She'd played him, used him, and manipulated him. He'd been a fool to believe that love existed. He'd never seen it—not the *love* they talk about in songs or in books. Not the look she'd given to Simon Johnson. None of it was real. It was a fictitious emotion created for saps who wanted to believe, an illusion—like Santa Claus. The *idea* brought people joy, until they were faced with the bitter reality and disappointment of betrayal. Hadn't Tony learned the truth a long time ago? Numbers were real. Money was real. Emotions were for the weak.

As the garage door closed, Tony reached for the ceramic cup. The liquid had cooled, yet as he used one hand to make the web conference fill his entire screen, his other hand tentatively touched the rounded handle as if it were potentially scalding. He didn't know how long it took to pick up the cup, or to take that first drink; however, as soon as he did, redness exploded, extreme pain clenched his chest, and blackness prevailed.

Chapter 12

Consequences were promised
—January 2012

(Consequences—after Chapter 46)

━━━━◆◆◆◆━━━━

Consequences are unpitying.
—George Eliot

VOICES INFILTRATED THE smothering darkness. Tony fought to find the surface, to break free of the blackness that surrounded him. It was as if he were at the bottom of a deep pit filled with water, swimming toward the air, pushing upward with all of his strength. *Where was it?* As the voices became clearer, he focused on and used them as his new goal. With all his might, he pushed toward the sound. A few more attempts and he'd break free.

The voices were clear. "Doctor, his vitals are stronger. The medicines have gotten his blood pressure back within the normal range."

"Have there been any signs of regaining consciousness?"

The first voice sounded less confident. "His physical response has been encouraging. The results of the EEG are in his chart, but we haven't had any signs of voluntary movement."

Tony pushed forward, *I'm here. I can hear you!* The darkness wouldn't allow him to speak. Unrelenting, it wrapped about him, filled him, and held him tight.

"Doctor, do we know the substance he ingested?"

"Not completely. The preliminary tests of the coffee found at the scene, and the contents removed from his stomach, confirm that the coffee was the source; however, due to his physical reaction, we believe the list is inconclusive."

"There was more than one toxin?"

"Yes, whoever did this, wanted to be sure it..."

The voices drifted farther away, taking with them Tony's audible goal and disorienting him in the darkness. Exhaustion prevailed and the blackness momentarily won.

TONY BLINKED HIS eyes, trying to focus on the world beyond the black. The room was bright, too bright, as people spoke. Keeping his eyes open was too difficult; instead, he settled into the darkness of his closed eyes and tried to listen. He heard voices, but their words were unfamiliar. Slowly they began to register... *his heart*—they were talking about his heart: it was beating.

That was reassuring, and he was glad to hear that, but he had to wonder: had it *not* been?

When he felt someone touch his forehead, he opened his eyes. It was one of the people in scrubs. Tony blinked toward her.

"Doctor, the patient is conscious."

Suddenly, another face was before him. This face had bright eyes that were acutely alert. "Hello, Mr. Rawlings, we're glad you decided to join us."

Tony tried to talk, but he couldn't. There were unknown

sensations in his chest and throat that ached. The sensation was more of discomfort than pain. He tried to block it and searched for a new goal. Somewhere in the chaos he found a consistent beeping—somewhere beyond the people and discomfort. Closing his eyes, he concentrated on the steady rhythm.

"Mr. Rawlings, don't leave us again. We need you to stay with us." It was the voice of the bright eyes.

He looked toward her and blinked.

"Can you hear me?"

Since he couldn't speak, he blinked.

"You had us all worried."

Tony's mind scrambled. *What happened? Where was he? Why were they talking about his heart?*

His heart.

They said it was beating, yet agonizing emptiness made him doubt its presence. As Bright Eyes stared, the memories rushed back. He couldn't think of anything except Claire's examination. She took the bait, drove away, and failed his test. How these people could possibly be right? How could his heart continue to beat when Claire had ripped it out of his chest and shattered it beyond repair?

Bright Eyes spoke again, "Mr. Rawlings, it seems that you ingested a poison. Do you remember what happened?"

He blinked again.

"You do? Did you take this toxin knowingly?"

He fought to keep his eyes open.

"Mr. Rawlings, relax. You'll be able to talk with us soon."

Soon? *Why couldn't he talk now?* Then there were people—more people—in his line of vision. They scrambled about pulling and prodding. He didn't want to think about what they were doing; instead he closed his eyes and listened to the beeps.

It was sometime later, the bright-eyed woman returned.

"Mr. Rawlings, can you speak?"

"Y-yes," he managed.

"Do you remember what you ingested?"

"Cof-coffee." His voice sounded unfamiliar—scratchy and weak.

"Yes, the police collected the coffee. It contained poison. The police want to talk to you. However, I believe you need your rest first. How are you feeling?"

"My chest and sides hurt."

Bright Eyes nodded. "We had to restart your heart. Whatever you ingested has had a negative effect on your heart muscle. We'll have to ensure that there's no permanent damage. We have a cardiologist who'll be in to talk with you regarding future treatment."

Tony blinked and tried to concentrate. "Treatment? What do you mean? There could be long-term effects from this?"

"I don't want to worry you unnecessarily, but yes. Mr. Rawlings, you're lucky to be alive—to have survived this. I'm guessing that either you were too healthy for this toxin, or the dose was misjudged."

"Are you saying that I could have died?"

Bright Eyes smiled. "I'm saying that you'll survive, and if treatment is necessary to facilitate that, we'll find what is best for you. In the meantime, the Iowa City Police have stationed officers outside of your door."

"Why?"

"Mr. Rawlings, someone tried to harm you. We don't want to give that someone another opportunity."

"I have my own security. I don't need policemen outside my door," Tony said.

"You can discuss that with the ICPD but not right now. I'm going to give you something to rest."

Tony looked around the room and saw the source of the repetitive beeping. "Nurse, what is all of this? Why is it beeping faster? Where's my doctor?"

Bright Eyes' smile returned. "First, your IV is flushing your body with fluid. It's helping to rid your blood and organs of the toxins. These are monitors that tell us what's happening inside of you. The one beeping faster is telling me that you are stressed, and the medication we just added to your IV will help alleviate that. Your heart doesn't need any unnecessary stress."

She had no fuck'n idea!

Tony tried to sit up, but Bright Eyes' small hand pushed against his shoulder. He couldn't believe that this tiny woman could overpower him. He'd never felt so weak. "Mr. Rawlings, listen to me. You need to rest. Let me introduce myself: I'm your doctor, Doctor Logan, and I want you to follow my rules."

His eyes opened wide. "Oh... I didn't realize. I just assumed... oh shit... I should probably just shut up."

Doctor Logan smiled again. "Yes, Mr. Rawlings, I think that would be a good idea. Soon the medicine will take effect and you'll feel sleepy. I recommend you rest. Then, when you wake, we'll see about you talking to the police."

"D-doctor?" His words began to slur.

"Yes, Mr. Rawlings?"

"W-where's my... wife?" Tony slipped back into the darkness.

The next time Tony woke, he wasn't alone. Eric was sitting in a recliner near his bed, reading a magazine. After a few swallows to moisten his throat, Tony found his voice. "Eric, why are you here? What happened to Claire?"

Eric dropped the magazine and moved swiftly to Tony's bedside. "Mr. Rawlings, um, Mrs. Rawlings is on her way back to Iowa City."

Tony's chest ached. He didn't know if the pain was from the

medical treatment or the confirmation in Eric's voice. "How far, Eric? How far did she drive?"

"Mr. Rawlings, I'm here to assure your safety."

"Are the police still outside?" When Eric looked puzzled, Tony continued, "The doctor, she told me about them—before."

"Yes, sir, they are. There're some FBI agents here too. I promised I'd alert them as soon as you woke. Do you want me to get them?"

"Eric, damn it! Answer my question. When Claire left the estate, how far did she go?"

Eric leaned forward and lowered his voice. "Sir, I don't believe the FBI want me to say anything."

"Since when do I give a fuck about anyone else's directives?"

Still whispering, Eric said, "Mr. Rawlings, Mrs. Rawlings was found, and she's been arrested in connection with your attempted murder."

Tony closed his eyes. Everything was in motion. It had proceeded just as they'd planned, and damn, his plans never failed. Well, once, but that was over—Claire finished it. Opening his eyes, he stared. "Go tell the damn police or FBI or whoever the fuck wants to listen, I'm ready to answer their questions."

During the few moments that Tony lay alone in his hospital room, he remembered a scene in Claire's suite. It was before they were married. They'd been discussing the prenuptial agreement. He remembered telling Claire why there wouldn't be an agreement. He said it was because they would not divorce—he would not leave her, and she would not leave him. He asked her if she knew what would happen if she did. She said she did.

As the law enforcement officers entered his room, Tony pushed the button, raised the back of his bed, and squared his shoulders. He bet Claire had no fuck'n idea of the consequences of her failure! She would soon find out what would happen!

———————◆———————

ANTHONY RAWLINGS' STATEMENT was straightforward. "There was nothing special about the morning. I got up, worked out in my gym, showered, ate breakfast, and began working."

"Working?" the officer asked.

"Yes, that's what I do—I work."

"Mr. Rawlings, did you go to your office?"

Tony pressed his lips together and momentarily stared. "Officer, I may be lying in a hospital bed, but I'm not crazy or stupid. Don't ask me questions when you already know the answers. I don't deal with incompetents and I don't intend to start."

The man bristled in his seat and rephrased his question. "Could you please be more specific about where you were working?"

"I have an office in my home. On occasion, I work from there. On the morning in question, I was working from my office within my home."

"Sir, who else was in your home?"

"My wife and my staff." Tony shook his head. "No one unusual."

"Did—" The officer immediately rephrased, "What did you eat and drink that morning?"

Tony tried to recall. "I had a bottle of water after my workout. I think I ate eggs and bacon for breakfast. There might have been fruit, I don't remember." He paused. "Oh, I had orange juice and coffee with breakfast."

"Was that all?"

"I had coffee again in my office, late in the morning."

The officer's shoulders stiffened. "Did you get your own coffee?"

"No." Tony didn't offer more.

"Sir, how do you take your coffee?"

"Black—sometimes with cream."

The man wrote more in his notepad. "Who brought your coffee to your office?"

"My wife," Tony mumbled.

"Did you say it was your wife?"

"Yes, my wife, Claire Rawlings, brought me coffee that morning, but if you or anyone else is suggesting that she would knowingly try to poison me, I believe you're mistaken."

It wasn't the young officer taking notes who responded. It was the older gentleman who'd been watching from the perimeter of the hospital room. "Mr. Rawlings, we aren't suggesting anything. We're trying to gather the evidence."

Tony was obviously feeling much stronger. Dr. Logan had been in earlier and authorized the questioning, and the cardiologist was scheduled to visit later in the afternoon. Tony leaned forward. "I'm at an obvious disadvantage," he spoke to the older gentleman. "You know my name, but I don't believe we've been introduced."

"Agent Hart, FBI."

"Well, Agent Hart, would you mind sharing that evidence with me?"

"Once our questioning is complete, we'll be glad to share with you. First, we want to know what you remember."

"I remember being with my wife the night before the morning in question. I remember a lot about that night and none of that would hint toward hostility. I'd share more, but out of respect for my wife, I won't. I remember talking with her on multiple occasions during the morning and making plans for later in the day. I remember booking a surprise vacation for the two of us. We're supposed to be in the Grand Caymans right now. I remember asking her for a cup of coffee and her bringing it. Tell me now, why you believe the woman I share my name and my bed with is being suspected of this crime."

Agent Hart nodded toward the young officer who'd been asking questions and taking notes. The younger man gathered his things and left the room. Once alone, Agent Hart swung the officer's chair around and straddled the seat. Leaning forward on the chair's back, he spoke quietly. "Mr. Rawlings, your wife was found yesterday driving near St. Louis."

He appeared genuinely shocked. Eric hadn't told him her destination. "St. Louis? Why?"

"Yes, Mr. Rawlings, why? Why would your wife leave your home in such a rush as to not take a coat? It is, after all, January in Iowa. Why would she leave without a purse, without her ID, and without any cash or credit cards?"

Tony couldn't respond if he'd wanted to. *St. Louis! She'd really left him. She'd taken the car and driven as far as she could.* Finally, he asked, "How did you find her?"

"Her car has built-in GPS. Your driver was kind enough to share the information, and we were able to track the vehicle."

"What did she say?"

"She hasn't said much. She's denied harming you, vehemently."

Tony closed his eyes. "Where is she? I want to talk to her."

"She's on her way back to Iowa." Agent Hart looked at his watch. "She may be back. The Iowa City prosecutor has secured a warrant for her arrest, and she's being arraigned this afternoon."

Shaking his head, Tony worked to contain the swirl of emotion: disappointment, betrayal, anger, hurt. It was a potent mixture. "I believe I need to speak with my legal team."

"Yes, Mr. Rawlings, I believe you do." Agent Hart stood. "I'll ask your driver to come back, if you'd like?"

"Agent?" Tony's voice hardened. "I don't want to believe any of this."

"I understand."

"I doubt you do. No matter what, find out who did this, and I want that person to pay. There has to be consequences for this. Do you understand?"

"Yes, sir, that I can assure you, I understand."

Once Agent Hart was gone and Eric was back, Tony began making calls. His first was to Tom. Tom and Brent headed up Tony's and Rawlings Corporation's legal team. Tony told Tom that under no circumstance would any of his legal team be used to defend Mrs. Rawlings.

Tony said, "If she did this to me, I don't intend to throw her a lifeline—she sure as hell didn't throw one to me!"

Chapter 13

It is MY decision—January 2012

(Consequences—Chapter 48)

———◦◦◦◆◦◦———

When a good man is hurt, all who would
be called good must suffer with him.
—Euripides

WITH EACH DAY that passed and Tony wasted in the hospital, his disappointment grew and festered. Every hour of work lost, every time someone entered his private room and performed some duty that was not to his liking, every time his personal space was invaded or the police came with more questions—every minute of each day was a reminder of how Claire had failed. Her failure didn't only affect her—no, Tony suffered as well.

He suffered physical pain as the toxins exited his body. Every time Tony took a deep breath or moved, he suffered piercing pain from the repercussions of the CPR. Two of his ribs were broken along with excessive damage to the cartilage in his chest. Then, there was the psychological suffering as he endured the humiliation of test after examination after test. Never had he been so exposed to so many people. Even his money couldn't save him from the prying eyes and hands of doctor after doctor.

After he regained his strength, Tony convinced the Iowa City Police Department and the FBI that he was safe with the help of his own security team. He explained that it was senseless for the people of Iowa to be burdened with the financial responsibility of his protection. The powers that be agreed, and Tony was at least free of the twenty-four-seven prying eyes of law enforcement.

The Simmonses cut their vacation short and hurried to Tony's bedside. Although he was happy to see them, they entered his hospital room right after Tony had finished another round of examinations and blood draws. His demeanor was not pleasant.

Their expressions were a mix of sadness and exhaustion. The trip from Fiji to Iowa had been long. Courtney was the first to speak as she rushed to Tony and swallowed him in a hug. He flinched at the discomfort. With tears in her eyes she said, "Oh, Tony, thank God! We've been so worried about you."

Brent gently slapped Tony's shoulder. "Hey, we rushed home because you're supposed to be at death's door. You look good to me."

"You missed the good part," Tony replied. "Apparently, I was more than at death's door—I passed the threshold. The doctors said they had to restart my heart."

Tears flowed from Courtney's eyes as she hugged him again. "Oh! I can't believe this. What happened? With all the traveling, we've only heard small snippets."

Brent cleared his throat. "We heard that Claire's been arrested. Man, tell us that isn't true."

Tony sat straighter and watched *his* best friends. "It is."

"No!" Courtney stood. "Claire wouldn't do this! There has to be some mistake."

"Do I look like there's a mistake?"

Using the voice Tony had heard in courtrooms and conference

negotiations, Brent said, "Courtney, let's hear what happened before jumping to any conclusions."

"She poisoned me!" Tony lowered his volume. "In front of a live web conference, I took a drink of coffee that Claire brought to me and I died! My damn heart stopped. Last I heard that's the definition of death. The police have reviewed all of my in-house surveillance and everything points to her. Marcus Evergreen has been here a couple of times. They have Claire locked up." When neither of his friends commented, Tony added, "She's being held on charges of *attempted* murder. Apparently, even though my heart stopped, the fact it restarted gets her out of a murder rap."

Brent wrapped Courtney in his arms as she hugged her midsection and her shoulders shuddered. Finally, she broke free and asked, "Why? Why would she do this? What happened? What did you do?"

Tony stared as red seeped into his peripheral vision. First, there were the damn doctors who poked and prodded, and now Courtney had the audacity to accuse him! It was all he could do to keep his lips pressed together in a tight line. When he looked away from Courtney, his eyes met Brent's. By his friend's expression, Tony believed that Brent knew what he was thinking. Tony didn't intend to say too much in front of Courtney, but he sure as hell would tell Brent.

Taking a deep breath, Tony winced and said, "I've spoken with Tom. No Rawlings money will be used for her defense. That means personal or corporate. No members of the Rawlings legal team will assist her, and that includes *you*," he looked to Brent, "and *your wife*."

Courtney shook her head and turned away.

Tony went on. "I personally hope that a trial can be avoided. I hardly want the world to know that I married a psycho who wanted me dead... nevertheless, the evidence is straightforward. I believe we should start thinking about a divorce."

"Tony, please," Courtney pleaded. "Please think about this. Please don't make decisions that you'll regret."

"Brent, I'd like to speak with you privately." Tony had never treated Courtney with anything other than respect. He didn't want to start now. To facilitate that—to avoid a possible confrontation, Tony needed her to leave. "Courtney, I've had nothing to do for the last few days but lie in this bed and think. I've thought this out multiple different ways. You two have been traveling and are obviously exhausted. I promise this was not a rushed decision. Now, I'd like to speak to Brent for a moment."

Brent nodded to Courtney as she picked up her coat and purse and headed toward the door. Just before she reached the handle, she said, "Tony, I'm really glad you're all right. You know how much we care about you, but you were the one who brought Claire into our lives. I don't abandon friends. Don't ask me to do that."

"I'm not. I'm asking you to support *me*."

Her shoulders lifted and dropped before she looked down and left the room.

Trying to keep his voice in check, Tony glared at Brent and waited for the door to shut. Once they were alone, he said, "Control your wife! That's not a recommendation nor a suggestion—I'm fuck'n serious. Claire did this to me. Neither you nor Courtney will visit or help her in any way!"

Brent nodded. "I hear you. Let me talk with Cort."

"Talk to her, do whatever you need to do, but I'm not backing down on this!"

Brent feigned a smile. "I guess we don't need to worry about you anymore. You're obviously feeling better."

Tony nodded. "Check in with Tom and get up-to-date. Evergreen seems to have everything under control, but I don't want a trial. I'm willing to do anything to avoid that. You know what I think about the damn press—they're already having a field day. I don't want to give them any more ammunition. I have no idea what my wife was thinking or why she did this. She'd been acting strangely since that old friend of hers died. Then, after she heard about John, she must have snapped."

"John?" Brent swallowed hard. "Did the shit hit the fan?"

"Yeah, a few days ago. His firm pressed charges."

Brent closed his eyes and shook his head. "Damn, I didn't know it would happen so soon."

"Focus! This isn't about him or even her. I'm getting out of here soon. Find out exactly what Evergreen's planning. He just trips over himself whenever I talk to him, with all his damn *yes sirs* and *no sirs*."

"I'll find out what's happening. Would you drop the charges to avoid a trial?"

"That's just it. I never pressed charges—the state of Iowa did. I fuck'n lost control of this, and I want you to get it back for me—yesterday."

Brent nodded and looked at his watch. "I'll see what I can do. Do you have your cell?"

"Yeah."

"I'll call you later tonight. When are they letting you out?"

"If I had my way it would've been yesterday. My doctor's this little five-foot firecracker who refuses to release me until some damn numbers drop in my blood."

Brent smiled. "So the administrators don't give a damn about your donations?"

"They do, and *they're* making sure I get the best. Apparently, that's her and she's not interested in my donations or cash on the side—I've tried. Maybe I should pay off the damn lab techs. I'll pay for the fuck'n numbers to go down."

"Jesus, Tony! Listen to the damn doctor. I'd bet they want you out of here as much as you want to be out."

Tony couldn't help but smile. "You're probably right, but I might look into the lab tech angle."

Brent walked toward the door. "I'm leaving. I'll call you after I talk with Evergreen."

"Brent." Tony's tone lowered. "Do what I said. Control your wife. Don't disappoint me."

Brent nodded as he stepped through the door. Tony saw members of his security staff standing just beyond the open frame. Closing his eyes, he remembered Catherine's words: *Claire and Mrs. Simmons were getting close?* Memories of Courtney's question increased his discomfort. *Close—how close?* Had Claire said anything to Courtney that would cause her to suspect him of pushing Claire to the extreme of attempted murder? Shit—he needed to feel that out. *Could it be that Claire had disappointed him without him even realizing it?* He opened his eyes. The monitor near his bed was beeping faster and faster as new red flooded the empty room.

———◆———

THE DAMN NUMBERS finally confirmed Tony's health. That didn't mean the pain was gone. His ribs hurt every time he breathed, and the cardiologist warned that Tony could have long-term effects. His heart would require further monitoring, but the signs for his long-range recovery were positive.

Riding up the drive of his estate, Tony pushed his emotions away. With Claire gone, his house seemed so empty. He'd spoken with Catherine on multiple occasions and, thankfully, she'd never boasted about Claire's failure. As a matter of fact, she was genuinely saddened by the outcome and worried about Tony's well-being. Whenever Tony mentioned Claire, Catherine would steer the subject to him and his recovery. He reassured her that he would get well, and he never doubted that he would.

Focusing on his responsibilities at Rawlings, which Tim had been assuming for too long, Tony entered his front door determined to ignore the obvious emptiness. His staff fell over themselves as they fulfilled his every need. It wasn't until he'd been home for a few hours that he wandered into the sitting room. He didn't mean to look above the fireplace—but he did. Tony wasn't looking for the green eyes; however, when he saw the large mirror that had hung there for years, fury overtook his being.

"Where the hell is the wedding portrait?"

There was no one near; the house was as empty as it felt. When he screamed his question again, Cindy came running. "Mr. Rawlings, are you all right? Can I help you?"

"No! I'm not all right! Where is Mrs. Rawlings' portrait?" He'd paid a fortune to have that portrait commissioned. He'd purposely had it painted by Sophia Rossi. No, not Rossi—Burke, and now it was gone!

"Sir, Catherine had it removed. She believed that you wouldn't—"

"I don't care what she believed! Where is it?"

"Sir, I-I don't know?"

"Where is Catherine?"

Suddenly, Catherine appeared, hurrying in from the hall. "Cindy, I'll help Mr. Rawlings. Thank you."

Cindy looked to Tony and waited. When he nodded, she turned away.

Catherine's voice tried to reassure. "Mr. Rawlings, you are supposed to rest."

He waited until Cindy left the room. "Where the fuck is the picture?"

"I thought that you—"

He glared. "I didn't ask you what *you* thought. I don't care what *you* think! Tell me where the fuck the painting is!"

Catherine's shoulders squared. "It's in her suite."

Tony closed his eyes and exhaled. Reestablishing his glare, he spoke slowly. "Don't you fuck'n touch any of her things. Don't make any damn assumptions about what I want and what I don't want. This isn't negotiable. Her things belong to me. Only I will decide what happens to them. I don't want to have this conversation again—ever. Are we clear?"

"Yes, sir." He heard the contempt in Catherine's voice, and at that moment Tony didn't give a damn.

"Have the portrait moved to my suite and hung over my fireplace. It'll stay there until I decide. Clear?"

"Yes, sir." He turned on his heel and stepped deliberately from the sitting room. Fighting the urge to go up to Claire's suite, Tony went to his office and contemplated his most recent revelation. If the state of Iowa wouldn't allow him to decide Claire's fate, then his most recent idea could. He called Brent.

Brent picked up on the third ring. "Yes, Tony?"

"What if she's insane?"

"Excuse me?"

"I told you that she'd been acting more and more detached since Johnson died. What if she lost it?"

Brent waited and then he said, "Evergreen said she's been very quiet, not saying much of anything."

Tony smiled. *This could work!* "If she pleads insanity, what could happen? Can we avoid the trial?"

"Let me look into it," Brent replied. "Do you want the state to sentence her to an institution?"

"No!" Tony's answer came too fast. "I want to pay for it. There's no sense having the people of Iowa pay her expenses."

"And when... *if*... she gets better?" Brent asked.

"We'll cross that bridge, but if I'm paying, it should be my decision." Everything about her had been his decision, even before she knew his name. He wasn't losing that control now.

"Tony, I'll investigate and get back to you. Evergreen said there's a preexamination scheduled for the day after tomorrow."

"I should be there."

"That isn't the customary practice."

"I don't give a shit what's customary. You investigate the insanity plea and I'll call Evergreen."

Tony didn't wait for Brent's answer before he hit: *DISCONNECT*.

TONY HAD JUDGE REYNOLDS' written decision in the breast pocket of his jacket. He didn't care if Evergreen didn't want him at this preexamination. Tony wanted Claire to plead insanity, and he needed to tell her. Honestly, he didn't expect any resistance from her or her counsel. Evergreen had said she received court-appointed attorneys, and apparently her draw hadn't been the best. Paul Task was fresh out of law school, had recently passed the bar, and was still wet behind the ears. His co-counsel was Jane Allyson. She'd spent a few years in the defender's office before and during law school. Evergreen said she was tenacious, but unestablished and unknown.

As Tony entered the hallway of conference rooms in the courthouse complex attached to the Iowa City jail, he was met by multiple law-enforcement officers. No one questioned his presence or commented about his wife's behavior. Everyone greeted him as if he were a long-lost friend. "Hello, Mr. Rawlings." "It's nice to see you, Mr. Rawlings." "Can I help you, Mr. Rawlings?"

It didn't take him long to find the conference room occupied by Evergreen and his team, as well as Claire and her legal team. There was a small window in the door. As soon as he looked in, he saw her. She looked so small and frail sitting at the cluttered table flanked by her incompetent counsel. Taking a deep breath, and remembering the pain of his broken ribs, he opened the door. The room, which had been full of murmuring, went silent. It was Marcus who finally stood and approached. "Mr. Rawlings, I thought we discussed this, and you weren't to attend this conference."

"Mr. Evergreen." Tony forced himself to look at the prosecutor as they shook hands. Every instinct in his body wanted to look at his wife. Feeling the green of her eyes penetrating his facade, he pushed on. "I appreciate everyone's concern for my safety. I'll repeat what I told Judge Reynolds. I don't believe my wife is a threat to my well-being. I believe if we can have a few moments alone, we can save the taxpayers of Iowa the cost of a lengthy trial, and this court, some time. Judge Reynolds has agreed to my request."

Marcus nodded and turned toward his team. Immediately, they began to move their chairs and stand. Claire's counsel whispered to one another and then to Claire. Next, Paul Task stood to meet Tony chest to chest. It was almost comical. Tony tried not to smile as Mr. Task stuttered, "M-Mr. Rawlings, I-I'll need to confirm that Judge Reynolds has indeed approved this visit. In situations such as this—"

Grinning, Tony reached into his jacket and passed a paper to Claire's frightened attorney. "Of course, Mr. Task. I would have expected no less. Here's the good judge's written approval."

Tony tried not to notice Paul Task's shaking hands as he took the paper and began to read. Once he was done, Tony smugly nodded as Claire's attorney turned toward her and confirmed, "Mrs. Rawlings, it appears to be in order."

As most of the room's occupants began to leave, Claire's co-counsel sat unmoving. Tony's gaze centered on the woman to Claire's right. Finally, Jane rose and met Tony's eyes. "Mr. Rawlings."

"Ms. Allyson." They nodded.

"Mr. Rawlings, this is unexpected. I'd like to speak to our client for a few moments and determine *her* desire regarding this meeting. If you'd please step into the hall with Mr. Evergreen and his team, Mr. Task and I will discuss this new situation with Mrs. Rawlings." *Who the hell did this woman think she was?* Tony started to respond, but Jane continued, "And then *if* Mrs. Rawlings agrees to your meeting, it may proceed under her conditions."

Before Tony could speak, Marcus placed his hand on Tony's arm and nodded. Tony turned toward Claire. This woman thought that she could stop him? He didn't need words, not with Claire. He wanted Claire to know that soon they'd be speaking, it wasn't open for debate. When he saw her expression, Tony's cheeks rose and his grin grew. She understood his unspoken promise. He turned back to her co-counsel. Accommodatingly, he said, "Why of course, Ms. Allyson," and stepped from the small room.

Once in the hallway, Marcus looked him in the eye and took a step backward. "I'm sorry, Mr. Rawlings, this is highly unusual. Ms. Allyson is—"

Tony squared his shoulders and smiled affirmatively. "—doing her job. I respect that, but as I've stated, I'm not frightened of my wife. I believe she was merely overwhelmed."

Marcus looked at his colleagues and then back to Tony.

Tony had everyone's attention. "You see, I've given this a lot of thought. Despite the evidence, I don't believe my wife wanted to kill me. The doctor said that the dose was wrong, and she's too intelligent for that. I'm a busy man. Perhaps it was nothing more than a cry for help."

"Mr. Rawlings, the state of Iowa—"

Tony put his hand on Marcus's shoulder. "The state of Iowa has done a remarkable job building a case. You've said that she's remained mostly silent. Is that still the case?"

Marcus nodded.

"Very well, I've had my attorneys working on this case day and night."

"But... it isn't up to *your* attorneys." Marcus answered, somewhat puzzled.

"No, it isn't. However, if..." Tony turned to address the entire group, "...if my wife pleads insanity—we can call it *temporary*. If my wife pleads temporary insanity and the state accepts that plea, I believe she'll receive the treatment she needs and deserves. Mrs. Rawlings isn't a criminal: she's ill. I want her to get the best care possible."

Marcus looked confused. "But, we have a solid case."

"I'm sure you do. I'm sure it wouldn't hurt your career, or any of your careers, to add this gem to your résumé. I can assure you though, that supporting the insanity defense, keeping this out of court, and allowing my wife to enter a private treatment facility, will also benefit your careers. You have my word."

Tony glanced toward the small window and saw Jane Allyson talking as Claire nodded. He wanted in that damn room.

"You realize," Marcus said, "it isn't enough for her to plead insanity. It must be clinically verified."

Tony grinned. "Yes, Marcus, I realize that. I have a plethora of psychiatrists ready to evaluate her."

"We have state-appointed—"

Before he could finish, Tony said, "I have their names, and I can assure you, they're on my list."

"It's customary for the courts to determine the amount of time and treatment—"

The door opened and Paul Task and Jane Allyson stepped from the room, interrupting their discussion. "Mr. Rawlings," Mr. Task said, "Mrs. Rawlings is ready to speak with you now."

Tony's smile broadened. "There are always exceptions, Marcus. I know this can be worked out."

Marcus Evergreen nodded as Tony stepped from the hall to the room. Closing the door behind him, he stared at his wife. Her eyes watched his every move. He sat down across the table from her. Bravely, she reached out and said, "Tony, I'm so glad you are all right." He took her petite hands in his and felt their coldness. For a moment he wanted to warm her, then she continued, "You know I'd never hurt you?"

He fought the red. *She'd left him. Driven to St. Louis. Made a public laughingstock of their marriage!* He tempered his tone. "My dear Claire, it certainly appears you did. You handed me the coffee. There was poison in the coffee."

"You told me to get you coffee." Although her voice was strong, he saw the tears that threatened to spill from her glistening eyes. She continued, "I've thought about it a million times. There must've been poison in the coffee already... or in the cream. I just don't know. I don't know who would do this. The only other people at home were staff—staff you've employed for years—but it should be on surveillance. You have cameras in the kitchen—"

He interrupted, "All evidence points to you. Then, there's the way you ran to the car and drove away."

Suddenly, the emerald was gone as she looked down at the table and mumbled, "I'm sorry." She paused. Still looking at the table, she continued, "It was impulsive. I knew not to take one of the cars, but I saw the keys. I hadn't had the opportunity in so long, the sky was so blue, and you'd been—well, life had been unpredictable. I felt like I was suffocating and just needed a reprieve, a small break. Honestly, Tony, I was about to turn around to come home. I wanted to be home—I want to be with you."

He lifted her chin. "Claire, how are your accommodations?" His voice was low yet strong. "Consequences, appearances, I thought you'd learned your lessons better."

"Tony, please take me home. I promise I'll never disappoint you again. Please tell them you know I wouldn't—*couldn't*—do this."

It was the pleading he wanted, and once she was in the mental facility, he'd allow her to expand upon her remorse. In the meantime, he needed to push forward.

Claire continued, "I know there'll be consequences and punishment. I don't care, as long as you're all right. I just want to go home. Please, please, Tony, they'll listen to you."

He looked deep into her eyes. He'd trusted her and she'd failed him. He spoke softly, "The entire thing seems to be a colossal *accident*. However, I've done some research and it seems you can plead insanity and receive *treatment* instead of *incarceration*."

She sprung from her chair and started to pace. "What are you saying? I'm not pleading insanity! That means guilty and crazy—I'm neither! And this wasn't an *accident*. I didn't try to kill you!"

He stood and moved very close. Looking down, he whispered, "Claire, listen. I've found a mental hospital that is willing to accept you. I'll pay the expenses so the taxpayers aren't responsible for your lack of judgment."

"I've been here for over a week. I've been questioned over and over. I haven't divulged any private information. I've followed all the rules. The only rule I broke was driving a car. That's it!"

She was too loud. He kept his voice low, trying to make her understand. "This plea will avoid a trial. The entire unfortunate incident is understandable. You came from a modest background. The life we shared had pressures and responsibilities—with entertaining, charities, and reporters. It's understandable. You just couldn't handle it."

Claire sat. Tony walked to her and bent down to maintain eye contact. "I should've recognized the signs. Perhaps, I was too busy with work. When you recently canceled your charity obligations, I should've realized how overwhelmed you felt." He fought the disappointment that fueled an unneeded rage. Although he tried to sound reassuring, authority prevailed in his tone. This was too important. Claire needed to listen to every word. It was what he'd done after her accident; he planted the seed and she obediently embedded its roots. He wanted the same outcome. Just as she'd responded to Dr. Leonard, he needed her to respond to her attorneys. "You wanted out, and in a moment of weakness—no, in a moment of *insanity*— you decided the only way out was to try to kill me. I'm only thankful that you underestimated the amount of poison needed or you may have succeeded. After all, if you'd succeeded, I wouldn't be here to help you now." He pulled out a chair and sat facing his wife. "Aren't you glad I'm able to help you? And, Claire..." He leaned nearer. "...I hear the rooms at the mental facility are larger than the cells at the federal penitentiary."

Tony expected a sign of recognition. He expected her to grab the lifeline he was throwing and hold on with both hands. It was a gift. She'd disappointed him—failed his test, publicly and privately—yet instead of walking away, he was offering her an out. This solution would help her and fulfill his need for control. Claire was his—her belongings, her portrait, and most importantly, her. He was angry. She had a long way to go to earn back his trust, but nonetheless, he was offering her an out. Claire needed to understand that he was helping her.

When she straightened her neck and met his eyes, he immediately realized—she wasn't taking his offer. The fire he loved to see was burning a blaze brighter than he'd ever seen. Didn't she understand? He loved that strength, but now wasn't the time. Now she needed to redeem herself.

Tony stood in amazement of the defiance before him. He wouldn't beg her! *Damn her.* This was crucial! He continued, disappointment audible in his tone, "Utilize the time you have to think this over. Don't make another poor, impulsive decision. This is your best offer." He knocked on the door. "Goodbye, Claire."

She didn't respond as he stepped back into the hall.

"Mr. Rawlings?" Marcus asked. "Is everything set?"

Counselor Allyson spoke, "This decision cannot be made without our input."

Tony turned toward the outspoken attorney. "Then I suggest that you convince your client that *she* has been offered a gift, and *she* should take it." With that, he nodded and walked down the hallway, leaving the group momentarily silent. The voice in his head cursed Claire's independence and stubbornness, pushing Tony to walk faster and faster.

Damn her! Damn her! A reprieve? A small break? Claire had left him! And now she was being obstinate!

Tony reasoned that she just needed time to consider his offer. A grin emerged as he reached the door of the courthouse. Yes, *time,* that was what she needed, time alone to think.

It had worked before. It would work again.

Epilogue

Damage control—Two days later
—January 2012

(Consequences—Chapter 49)

———◆———

Reputation is rarely proportioned to virtue.
—Saint Francis de Sales

"Mr. Rawlings, Mr. Evergreen is calling." Patricia's voice came through the speaker.

Tony turned away from the computer screen. "I'll take it."

"Yes, sir, I'll send it through."

It had been two days since Tony had visited the courthouse, two days since he'd given Claire the gift of an out. He knew she was upset at the time, but he had faith that her better judgment would eventually prevail. This was the first he'd heard from the prosecutor since that afternoon.

"Marcus, I assume you have some good news for me."

Marcus Evergreen cleared his throat. "Um, not exactly, Mr. Rawlings."

Tony's grip tightened on the receiver, yet his tone remained affable. "Would you like to be more specific?"

"Can you come to my office?"

Tony contemplated his schedule. He'd already wasted too much of his time on this whole mess. "I just returned back to my work, and things are backed up. Are you sure this can't be handled over the phone or by email?"

"Well, I think... see... I believe it would be in your best interest—"

"Marcus, spit it out. Time is money."

"Mr. Rawlings, j-just moments ago, I received Paul Task's preliminary brief. I haven't had a chance to read the entire document. It's quite long, but I've read enough—"

Tony interrupted, "Tell me that she's taking my offer."

"That's the thing, sir. She isn't. She's made allegations..." Marcus continued to speak, but his words faded into the buzz of seeping crimson. "...why I thought you might prefer if I didn't email this?"

"Marcus, I told you she was crazy. This is ridiculous!"

"Do you want me to email—"

"No! I don't want you to email or show it to another soul! I'll be there in less than thirty minutes." Tony hung up the phone before Marcus could respond.

<hr/>

TONY CONTEMPLATED HIS response to whatever was in Claire's statement. As soon as Tony hung up with Marcus, he called for Eric. When he learned that Eric was at the estate, Patricia willingly offered her car. The entire drive, Tony's mind was on Claire. *What had she said? Would she really divulge private information?* His leather gloves strained from the grip on the poor car's steering wheel. He wouldn't allow this information to go public. Hell, he didn't even want his attorneys to be involved. Tony debated his options.

Taking a deep breath he entered the prosecutor's office. It bustled with people—men and women in suits coming and going all different directions. Mr. Evergreen's secretary, a young blonde woman with a nameplate that read Kirstin, stood at the ready. As soon as she saw Mr. Rawlings, she immediately escorted him to the unimpressive office. Marcus stood as Tony entered, and the two momentarily stared in silence. The frightened young lady took one last look at the two men and backed out quietly, shutting the door and allowing them their privacy.

Once alone, Marcus offered his hand and began somewhat sheepishly, "Thank you for hurrying over. I realize you have a very busy schedule."

Tony shook the prosecutor's hand and stared intently. "Tell me, who else has seen this testimony?"

"It isn't really testimony. It wasn't said under oath." Marcus shook his head as he walked around his desk and motioned to a small table. "Please, have a seat. No one on my team has seen it. Only me."

"On your team?" Tony asked, as he laid his overcoat on one chair and sat.

"Paul Task and Jane Allyson obviously took Mrs. Rawlings' statement," Marcus replied. "I don't know who prepared the document."

"Find out."

Marcus nodded. "Mr. Rawlings, there're some serious allegations. Legally this should be forwarded to—"

Tony sat back against the chair and squared his shoulders. "If you planned to do that, you wouldn't have called me."

"It's just," the prosecutor began, "I don't want the mad ravings of an angry spouse to bring down the reputation of such an esteemed man, such as yourself."

"Thank you, Marcus. I appreciate your candor and your discretion."

"Would you like to read what she's said?" Marcus asked as he booted up his laptop.

Tony shook his head. "No... to be honest, I wouldn't. It saddens me. I can't imagine what she's said, but it must be something terrible for you to have been this concerned."

"It isn't flattering," Marcus admitted.

"I don't want this made public." Tony's tone was not up for debate. "I don't want anyone to know that the woman I married has become delusional and irrational." Tony leaned forward. "I'm sure you've seen the media coverage. Let's not add to the frenzy."

"I totally understand. If only she'd have taken your offer—"

"Obviously," Tony said, "another sign of her mental incompetency. I want you to do whatever it takes to keep this out of a courtroom."

Marcus nodded. "Sir, some of these allegations seemed very farfetched. May I ask if your wife had access to others?"

Tony's brows came together. "What kind of a question is that? This's 2012—everyone has access to everyone."

"Cell phone? Email?"

Tony nodded. "Yes," he sounded puzzled, "doesn't everyone?"

"May I have her number and email address?"

"Yes, of course. Whatever you need, I'll be glad to provide. I'm sure you can find many things just by searching the media. They do seem to like to write about my wife's latest purchases... or... hair color." Tony looked down.

"Mr. Rawlings, I apologize. I'm sure this is extremely difficult. It's that, we'll be meeting with Mrs. Rawlings and her attorneys in the morning. The more prepared I am for this preexamination, the better chance we have of stopping this from going to full trial."

Tony took a deep breath; his ribs ached. He reached for his side, and said, "I suppose this'll get worse before it gets better."

"I'll be in touch. I promise to keep you up-to-date."

Tony stood, his dark eyes downcast before settling on the prosecutor. "Marcus, I promise that you'll not regret this. I know you won't disappoint me, and I won't disappoint you. The state of Iowa has excellent opportunities. I believe there are great prospects in your future."

Marcus's shoulders went back. "Thank you, Mr. Rawlings. I'm truly saddened by this string of events. I'll keep the casualty list as short as possible."

"Tony," Tony said. "Please, you've been to my wedding and by my side as it all fell apart. Please, call me Tony."

"Thank you, Tony. I'll also let you know the full list of who's seen this information and promise to keep that list manageable."

Tony put out his hand. "I don't doubt your abilities. That's why I believe you have true possibilities for great aspirations. Both of our futures will be much brighter. I look forward to hearing from you."

Tony gathered his overcoat and stepped from Marcus' office, confident of the containment of Claire's disobedience. Fine! She didn't want to take his offer. Tony wouldn't be derailed by a Nichols! Let her rot in a damn prison. Let her experience the consequences of her decision—at least Tony would know where she was. One day her little reprieve would be over, and she'd be free—from the state of Iowa, that was, but never from him.

Tony could promise that!

Above anything else, Anthony Rawlings was a man of his word.

⸺◆⸺

THE END... until *Behind His Eyes*—TRUTH

Glossary of Consequence Series Characters - Book #1 and #4

-Primary Characters-

Anthony (Tony) Rawlings: *billionaire, entrepreneur, founder of Rawlings Industries*

Anton Rawls: *son of Samuel, grandson of Nathaniel (birth name)*

Claire Nichols: *meteorologist/ bartender/ woman whose life changed forever*

-Secondary Characters-

Brent Simmons: *Rawlings Attorney/ Tony's best friend*

Catherine Marie London: *housekeeper/ friend of Anton Rawls*

Courtney Simmons: *Brent Simmons' wife*

Emily (Nichols) Vandersol: *Claire's older sister*

John Vandersol: *Emily's husband/ Claire's brother-in-law/ attorney*

Nathaniel Rawls: *grandfather of Anton Rawls/ father of Samuel Rawls/ owner of Rawls Corporation*

Samuel Rawls: *son of Nathaniel Rawls / father of Anton*

-Tertiary Characters-

Amber McCoy: *Simon Johnson's fiancée*

Amanda Rawls: *Samuel Rawls' wife, Anton's mother*

Anne Robinson: *Vanity Fair reporter*

Bev Miller: *designer, wife of Tom Miller*

Bonnie: *wife of Chance*

Brad Clark: *wedding consultant*

Caleb Simmons: *son of Brent and Courtney Simmons*

Carlos: *house staff at Rawlings estate*

Chance: *associate of Elijah Summer's*

Charles: *housekeeper, Anthony's Chicago apartment*

Cindy: *maid at the Rawlings estate*

Connie: *Nathaniel Rawls' secretary*

David Field: *Rawlings negotiator*

Elijah (Eli) Summers: *entertainment entrepreneur, friend of Tony's*

Eric Hensley: *Tony's driver and assistant*

Agent Hart: *FBI agent*

Agent Ferguson: *FBI agent*

Jan: *housekeeper, Anthony's New York apartment*

Jane Allyson: *court-appointed counsel*

Jared Clawson: *CFO Rawls Corporation*

Julia: *Caleb Simmons' fiancée*

Kelli: *secretary Rawlings Industries, New York office*

Kirstin: *Marcus Evergreen's secretary*

Marcus Evergreen: *Iowa City Prosecutor*

Mr. and Mrs. Johnson: *Simon Johnson's parents*

Dr. Leonard: *physician*

Dr. Logan: *physician*

MaryAnn Combs: *longtime companion of Elijah Summer, Tony's friend*

Meredith Banks: *reporter, sorority sister of Claire Nichols*

Sergeant Miles: *police officer, St. Louis*

Monica Thompson: *wedding planner*

Naiade: *housekeeper in Fiji*

Patricia: *personal assistant to Anthony Rawlings, Corporate Rawlings Industries*

Paul Task*: court-appointed counsel*

Judge Reynolds: *court judge, Iowa City*

Sharon Michaels: *attorney for Rawlings Industries*

Sharron Rawls: *wife of Nathaniel Rawls*

Shaun Stivert: *photographer for Vanity Fair*

Shelly: *Anthony Rawlings' publicist*

Simon Johnson: *first love and classmate of Claire Nichols, gaming entrepreneur*

Sophia Burke: *owner of art studio in Provincetown, Massachusetts*

Sue Benson: *Tim Benson's wife*

Tim Benson: *vice president, Corporate Rawlings Industries*

Tom Miller: *Rawlings Attorney, friend of Tony's*

The Consequences Series Timeline

---◆---

-1921-

Nathaniel Rawls—born

-1943-

Nathaniel Rawls—home from WWII

Nathaniel Rawls marries Sharron

-1944-

Samuel Rawls—born to Nathaniel and Sharron

-1962-

Catherine Marie London—born

-1963-

Samuel Rawls marries Amanda

-1965- (February 12)

Anton Rawls—born to Samuel and Amanda

-1975-

Rawls Corporation goes public

-1980-

Emily Nichols—born to Jordon and Shirley Nichols

-1983- (October 17)

Claire Nichols—born to Jordon and Shirley Nichols

-1986-

Rawls Corporation falls

-1987-

Nathaniel Rawls found guilty of multiple counts of insider trading, misappropriation of funds, price fixing, and securities fraud

-1989-

Nathaniel Rawls—dies

Samuel and Amanda Rawls—die

-1990-

Anton Rawls changes his name to Anthony Rawlings

Anthony Rawlings begins CSR-Company Smithers Rawlings with

Jonas Smithers

-1994-

Anthony Rawlings buys out Jonas Smithers and CSR becomes

Rawlings Industries

-1996-

Rawlings Industries begins to diversify

-2002-

Claire Nichols—graduates high school

Claire Nichols—attends Valparaiso University

-2004-

Jordon and Shirley Nichols—die

-2005-

Emily Nichols—marries John Vandersol

-2007-

Claire Nichols—graduates from Valparaiso, degree in meteorology

Claire Nichols—moves from Indiana to New York for internship

-2008-

Claire Nichols—moves to Atlanta, Georgia, for job at WKPZ

-2009-

WKPZ—purchased by large corporation resulting in lay-offs

-2010-

Anthony Rawlings—enters the Red Wing in Atlanta, Georgia (March)

Anthony Rawlings—takes Claire Nichols on a date

Claire Nichols—wakes at Anthony's estate

Claire Nichols—liberties begin to increase (May)

Anthony Rawlings—takes Claire Nichols to symphony and introduces "Tony" (late May)

Meredith Banks' article appears—Claire Nichols' accident

Anthony Rawlings—marries Claire Nichols (December 18)

-2011-

Vanity Fair article

Claire Rawlings—sees college boyfriend, Simon Johnson

Simon Johnson—dies

-2012-

Claire Rawlings—drives away from the Rawlings estate

Anthony Rawlings—poisoned

Claire Rawlings—arrested for attempted murder

Anthony Rawlings—divorces Claire Nichols

Claire Nichols—receives box of information while in prison

What to do now...

LEND IT: Did you enjoy BEHIND HIS EYES CONSEQUENCES? Do you have a friend who'd enjoy BEHIND HIS EYES CONSEQUENCES? BEHIND HIS EYES CONSEQUENCES may be lent one time. Sharing is caring!

RECOMMEND IT: Do you have more than one friend who'd enjoy BEHIND HIS EYES CONSEQUENCES? Tell them about it! Call, text, post, tweet... your recommendation is the nicest gift you can give to an author!

REVIEW IT: Tell the world. Please go to the retailer where you purchased this, as well as Goodreads, and write a review.

Stay connected with Aleatha

Do you love Aleatha's writing? Do you want to know the latest about Infidelity? Consequences? Tales From the Dark Side? and Aleatha's new series coming in 2016 from Thomas and Mercer?

Do you like EXCLUSIVE content (never released scenes, never released excerpts, and more)? Would you like the monthly chance to win prizes (signed books and gift cards)? Then sign up today for Aleatha's monthly newsletter and stay informed on all things Aleatha Romig.

Sign up for Aleatha's NEWSLETTER: http://bit.ly/1PYLjZW
(recipients receive exclusive material and offers)

You can also find Aleatha@

Check out her website: http://aleatharomig.wix.com/aleatha
Facebook: https://www.facebook.com/AleathaRomig
Twitter: https://twitter.com/AleathaRomig
Goodreads: goodreads.com/author/show/5131072.Aleatha_Romig
Instagram: http://instagram.com/aleatharomig
Email Aleatha: aleatharomig@gmail.com

You may also listen Aleatha Romig books on Audible.

Books by
NEW YORK TIMES BESTSELLING AUTHOR
Aleatha Romig

THE CONSEQUENCES SERIES:

CONSEQUENCES
(Book #1)
Released August 2011

TRUTH
(Book #2)
Released October 2012

CONVICTED
(Book #3)
Released October 2013

REVEALED
(Book #4)
Previously titled: Behind His Eyes Convicted: The Missing Years
Re-released June 2014

BEYOND THE CONSEQUENCES
(Book #5)
Released January 2015

COMPANION READS:

BEHIND HIS EYES—CONSEQUENCES
(Companion One of the bestselling Consequences Series)
Released January 2014

BEHIND HIS EYES—TRUTH
(Companion Two of the bestselling Consequences Series)
Released March 2014

TALES FROM THE DARK SIDE SERIES:

INSIDIOUS
(All books in this series are stand-alone erotic thrillers)
Released October 2014

DUPLICITY
(Completely unrelated to book #1)
Release TBA

THE LIGHT SERIES:
Published through Thomas and Mercer

INTO THE LIGHT
(June 14, 2016)

AWAY FROM THE DARK
(October 2016)

Aleatha Romig

Aleatha Romig is a New York Times and USA Today bestselling author who lives in Indiana. She grew up in Mishawaka, graduated from Indiana University, and is currently living south of Indianapolis. Aleatha has raised three children with her high school sweetheart and husband of nearly thirty years. Before she became a full-time author, she worked days as a dental hygienist and spent her nights writing. Now, when she's not imagining mind-blowing twists and turns, she likes to spend her time with her family and friends. Her other pastimes include reading and creating heroes/anti-heroes who haunt your dreams!

Aleatha released her first novel, CONSEQUENCES, in August of 2011. CONSEQUENCES became a bestselling series with five novels and two companions released from 2011 through 2015. The compelling and epic story of Anthony and Claire Rawlings has graced more than half a million e-readers. Aleatha released the first of her series TALES FROM THE DARK SIDE, INSIDIOUS, in the fall of 2014. These stand-alone thrillers continue Aleatha's twisted style with an increase in heat. In the fall of 2015, Aleatha moved headfirst into the world of romantic suspense with the release of BETRAYAL, the first of her five-novel INFIDELITY series. Aleatha has entered the traditional world of publishing with Thomas and Mercer with her LIGHT series. The first of that series, INTO THE LIGHT, will be published in the summer of 2016.

Aleatha is a "Published Author's Network" member of the Romance Writers of America and represented by Danielle Egan-Miller of Browne & Miller Literary Associates.

BCPL
Baltimore County
Public Library

CPSIA information can be obtained
at www.ICGtesting.com
Printed in the USA
LVOW10s1619110517
534160LV00004B/774/P